WAR IN
SANDOVAL COUNTY

WAR IN SANDOVAL COUNTY

WAYNE D. OVERHOLSER

THORNDIKE
CHIVERS

This Large Print edition is published by Thorndike Press, Waterville, Maine, USA and by BBC Audiobooks Ltd, Bath, England.

Thorndike Press, a part of Gale, Cengage Learning.

LIBRARY OF CONGRESS CATALOGING-IN-PUBLICATION DATA

Overholser, Wayne D., 1906–1996.
    War in Sandoval County / by Wayne D. Overholser.
        p. cm. — (Thorndike Press large print Western)
    ISBN-13: 978-1-4104-1867-8 (hardcover : alk. paper)
    ISBN-10: 1-4104-1867-7 (hardcover : alk. paper)
    1. Ranchers—Crimes against—Fiction. 2. Sandoval County
(N.M.)—Fiction. 3. Large type books. I. Title.
PS3529.V33W28 2009
813'.54—dc22   2009033900

BRITISH LIBRARY CATALOGUING-IN-PUBLICATION DATA AVAILABLE

Published in 2009 in the U.S. by arrangement with Golden West Literary Agency.
Published in 2010 in the U.K. by arrangement with Golden West Literary Agency.

U.K. Hardcover: 978 1 408 47712 0 (Chivers Large Print)
U.K. Softcover: 978 1 408 47713 7 (Camden Large Print)

Printed in the United States of America
1 2 3 4 5 6 7 13 12 11 10 09

WAR IN
SANDOVAL COUNTY

CHAPTER I

A line ran down the middle of Starbuck's Main Street, intangible but as effective as if it were made of barbed wire. On the south side were the Belle Union Saloon, Wellman's Store, and the Red Front Livery Stable. Their customers were the farmers and the small ranchers. Across the street the business places were patronized by the wealthier cowmen known locally as the Big 4. Jeff Ardell, riding in from his Rafter A, belonged to this group, but he kept his horse squarely in the middle of the street.

Jeff was one of the few men in the west end of Sandoval County who did business on both sides of the street. Now, with the sun just beginning to drop toward the western horizon, Jeff reflected on the stupidity and greed that had brought about this division. It had not existed when his father, Matthew Ardell, had been on his feet; it had started, as nearly as Jeff could tell, three years ago when Matthew had been kicked by a horse and relegated to a wheel chair.

A long line of horses were racked on the south side of the street but none on the north except Nikki Shortt's driving mare in front of the home of Miles Rebus, the preacher. That was far to the east at the edge of town, and didn't really count.

By tacit consent, the south side would be cleared by late afternoon, but after dark the hitch poles on the north side would be filled. In that way violence had been averted, but Jeff knew that it was a temporary expedient at best.

Jeff intended to buy a few things at Wellman's Store, then cross to the north side to pick up some medicine for his father at Doc Bennett's drugstore, and finally call at Miles Rebus' house by way of the back door to see Nikki Shortt. But when he was opposite the Belle Union, Lacey Dunbar stepped through the bat wings and called, "Jeff, come in and have a drink."

If it had been anyone but Dunbar, Jeff would have said no, but Lacey Dunbar was his best friend. So Jeff said, "Sure, Lacey." Finding a place at the end of the hitch rack to tie, he stepped down, looped the reins over the pole, and went in.

Fifteen or more men lined the bar, the

riffraff of the county according to Ben Shortt whose Wineglass was the biggest spread in the county. He was Nikki's grandfather, a relationship which had been decided by fate. That was Shortt's good luck, but not Nikki's. If she could have chosen her grandfather, she certainly wouldn't have picked Ben Shortt.

Dunbar slapped Jeff on the back. "Step up and order, son. Tom's buying."

Tom Barren, the first man in line, gave Jeff his meager grin. "Looks like I'm stuck," Barren said. "What'll it be?"

"Beer," Jeff said, his gaze ranging from Tom Barren's smooth-shaven, narrow face on to Red O'Toole's freckled one at the far end of the bar. All of them spoke or nodded, and then were silent, watching him with a kind of wary expectancy. Jeff brought his gaze back to Dunbar, asking, "Who's the funeral for?"

"All of us, looks like," Dunbar said.

The bartender served Jeff and then stood staring at him. Abe Wellman was here from the store next door. So was Barney Hollis who ran the Red Front Livery Stable. Necessity made strange bedfellows, Jeff thought.

Lacey Dunbar stood apart from the rest. He was a loner, a man who would not have been here under ordinary circumstances. He had no more ties with the others than Jeff Ardell did.

Dunbar ran a horse ranch on the other side of Deer Creek close to the Utah line. He worked for Jeff during roundup, but the rest of the time he lived alone. He wore his hair long, he hadn't shaved for years, and he seldom came to town except to buy a few necessities.

Jeff drank his beer, the silence sending a crawly feeling through him. Irritated, he said, "What'd you call me in for?"

"None of us know quite how to catch hold of it," Tom Barren said. "You're a nabob, but we're rustlers and thieves who have to be driven out of the county. Or so Ben Shortt says."

"You know I don't hold to that," Jeff said. "Ben's got a right to think what he wants to about you same as you can think what you want to about him."

Barren ran the tip of a finger over his carefully trimmed mustache. He was forty, slender and average tall, and was the nearest to a leader that these men had. A bachelor who lived alone on Deer Creek at the west end of Red Mesa, he was as prosperous as any of the ranchers who lived in the little valleys west of Red Mesa. He was a

10

good friend of the Ardells, often visiting at the Rafter A, but Jeff didn't like him. Jeff wasn't sure why he felt that way, but there was no doubt about his feeling.

"If you can't get hold of it, I can," Dunbar said, and pulling a crumpled sheet of paper out of his pocket, handed it to Jeff. "We all got 'em, son. To hell with you being a nabob. You ain't Ben Shortt's breed of dogs."

Floyd Deems, who owned the outfit below Barren's on Deer Creek, nodded. "Your dad is a good man, Jeff. He used to pull the string on Ben Shortt. Now we want to know what you aim to do."

"Nothing," Jeff said. "I'm not dad, Floyd."

He smoothed out the paper and read the note written in Ben Shortt's big, plain hand. "Sell out and get out of the county while you can. See me if you want a deal. Ben Shortt."

Jeff returned the paper to Dunbar. Funny how a man lived from day to day, knowing something was going to happen while all the time he was hoping it wouldn't happen, and then, when it did, be utterly unprepared for it.

"Any of you find out what kind of deal Ben will give you?" Jeff asked.

"No," Red O'Toole said angrily. He was

Deems's neighbor to the north, the most impetuous man in the room. "We ain't goin' to, neither. It ain't that any of us have got much, but it's our business whether we stay. We don't cotton to bein' shoved around by Ben Shortt."

"I had nothing to do with those letters," Jeff said.

"We know it," Barren said. "The point is every man in this end of the county has got to stand up and be counted. Where do you stand, Jeff?"

Sharpness was the word for Tom Barren. His nose was narrow and pointed. So was his chin. He was an expert at cutting a man's throat with his tongue without raising his voice. His eyes were light green, like ice without the slightest hint that someday they might thaw with human warmth.

Jeff had never given it much thought before, but now, staring at Barren, he sensed these qualities about the man and realized that they were the reasons he didn't like him. Even Ben Shortt, for all his greed and love of power, was not the cold and withdrawn man that Tom Barren was.

Jeff hesitated a moment, fighting the anger that Barren's blunt words aroused in him, and was defeated. He said, "I don't have to answer to you, Tom."

He would have walked out if Dunbar hadn't said, "A Wineglass hand delivered Shortt's message Friday. Yesterday morning, it was. What does Shortt aim to do? That's why we called you in."

"I don't know," Jeff said. "I'd tell you if I did."

"What about Steve Lawrence and Hank Dolan?" Floyd Deems asked. "Are they going to keep on using the same pot Shortt does?"

Lawrence and Dolan were the other members of the Big 4 and notorious yes men for Shortt. Jeff thought about Deems's question, wondering if Shortt had consulted them, or had he simply gone ahead with his plan, expecting to be backed up by the others?

"I don't know," Jeff said. "Shortt sent word to me yesterday to come to Wineglass tomorrow afternoon. I'll probably find out then what he's up to."

"We're all in this together," Abe Wellman said, troubled. "All the men in this room but you has an account at my store. If Ben Shortt runs everybody out he don't like, I'm busted."

"Shortt's been callin' us rustlers," O'Toole burst out, "and I'm gettin' tired of it. Maybe he has been losin' cattle, but I figure he's

13

usin' it as an excuse to get more range for Wineglass."

Lacey Dunbar snorted. "Well, Red, I like the flavor of Wineglass beef. So do you. I'll bet my bottom dollar you ain't butchered one of your own steers for five years."

"No sense of us claiming we eat our own beef," Barren said. "Shortt can afford to lose the few steers we eat, but he claims it's a big operation. If it is, I don't think any of us are in it."

In spite of his words, his tone held doubt, and Jeff sensed that the doubt was in all of them. They wouldn't hold together against Shortt, and that was exactly what the Wineglass owner was counting on. Some would stick even if it meant their death. Lacey Dunbar was one. Tom Barren was another. Red O'Toole might. The others would pull out at the first show of violence.

There was no sense in his staying here any longer. At the moment he was sure of just one thing. He didn't have to tell these men how he stood, but he'd tell Ben Shortt.

"I'll be moseying," Jeff said. "Got some chores to do."

He went out, not realizing that Barren was following until he was on the street in the hot June sunlight. Barren said in his precise tone, "Wait, Jeff. I want to talk to you."

14

Jeff turned back, impatient to be gone. He hadn't seen Nikki for a week, and he knew she had been expecting him for the past half-hour. They had been using the preacher's home as a meeting place for more than three months.

Nikki was almost eighteen, Jeff twenty-three. Neither was sure when they had fallen in love, but it had happened. Even Ben Shortt's dominating will couldn't alter the fact. They hadn't talked to him about it. No use. Nikki was his only living relative. He'd horsewhip any man who tried to take her from him.

"Well?" Jeff asked.

"I've been wanting to talk to you about something for quite a while," Barren said. "You know how it is with me. I've got a comfortable house and I live alone. I could increase the size of my herd if I had help. I've been thinking it would profit both of us if we threw in together."

"No."

"Now don't go off half-cocked," Barren protested. "Sooner or later you'll be in trouble with Shortt. When that time comes, he'll wipe you out just like he's aiming to do with us."

"He's seventy," Jeff said. "He won't live forever."

15

"He looks and acts like a man of fifty," Barren said. "He may outlive the bunch of us. I'm suggesting that your dad sell out to Shortt and the three of you live with me. In the end we'll make more than we're making now. If you make the move right away, we'll be in a better position to fight Shortt."

"I don't aim to fight him," Jeff said, and started to turn toward his horse.

Barren grabbed his arm. "Listen to me, damn it. Shortt doesn't have any more use for you than he does me or Lacey Dunbar. The only reason he wants you on his side is because your name's Ardell. Matthew made it mean something."

It was true, but hearing it from Tom Barren didn't make Jeff like it. He jerked free from Barren's grip, and mounting his horse, rode down the street. Why did Tom Barren think the Ardells would be crazy enough to move off Red Mesa and onto Deer Creek with the limited graze that was there?

Jeff shrugged and thought about Lacey Dunbar. Maybe he could get Dunbar to come to the Rafter A. No, Lacey wouldn't do that. He liked his way of life, lonely as it was. He'd never change.

Jeff turned it over in his mind, feeling utterly futile because there was nothing anyone could do for Lacey Dunbar.

16

CHAPTER II

Jeff turned off Main Street and came to Miles Rebus' house from the rear. He dismounted and leaving the reins dragging, started up the path toward the back door.

This was the way he and Nikki had been forced to meet all spring. She would leave her buggy in front as if she were calling on Mrs. Rebus, and he would ride around to the back. He'd go into the house and Mrs. Rebus would find something to do in the kitchen so he could be alone with Nikki in the parlor.

Sooner or later there would be a blow-up because someone was bound to tell Ben Shortt. Jeff was surprised that it hadn't happened before this. The only reason it hadn't, he thought, was that Ben Shortt was a hard man to tell anything.

Jeff heard Miles Rebus using a hoe to clean the dropboard in the chickenhouse. He turned off the path, and walking through

17

the weeds, called, "That you, Miles?"

"Sure is." The preacher stepped outside and leaned his hoe against the wall. "I didn't hear you ride up."

Jeff was always a little surprised at Miles. He didn't look or act the way other preachers had who had served the Starbuck church. For the first time in his life Jeff had become a regular church attendant simply because he liked and admired the man.

Rebus was stocky, with strong hands and arms and heavy-muscled shoulders, a full head shorter than Jeff. He was a good hay hand, and had worked for Jeff both summers he had been in Starbuck. In addition, he added to his meager salary by keeping two cows, more than one hundred Plymouth Rock hens, and raised the biggest garden on the mesa.

"I ride a silent horse," Jeff said. "Nikki here?"

"She's waiting for you," Miles answered, "but she'll wait another five minutes. I want to talk to you."

Jeff never had enough time for Nikki and he begrudged the five minutes Miles wanted, but he was never impatient with the preacher as he had been with Tom Barren. He said, "All right, but I may walk off at the end of five minutes."

18

Miles laughed. He was two or three years older than Jeff and had been married just a week before he came to Starbuck. "Get out your watch and see that I don't take more than five minutes." He glanced at Jeff, then looked away. "How big are your feet, Jeff?"

Jeff stared at his dust-covered boots. "What are you driving at?"

"Are your feet big enough to fill your dad's shoes?"

"No, they're not," Jeff said sharply. "I buy boots to fit my feet, not pa's."

"Of course," Miles said quickly. "I guess I didn't say it right. I never knew Matthew when he was able to get around, but I've heard a lot about him. He never wore a gun and he doesn't believe in violence, yet there was very little violence here in a new country where you would expect it. There would have been if Matthew hadn't lived here. I've often wondered how he did it."

"I don't know," Jeff said, "except that he had more sand in his craw than any other man I ever knew. One time I saw him walk up to a drunk who was going to kill him and take the gun away from him. I couldn't have done it."

"I couldn't, either," Miles said. "But that's behind us. He lost his power the day he was hurt. Now all that is bad in Ben Shortt's

19

coming out in him. This is murder, Jeff, and I can't do anything except stand here and watch it happen."

"You mean the order he's given Tom Barren and the rest?"

"No. I didn't know about that."

Jeff told him, then asked, "What did you mean?"

Miles hesitated, then he said, "I shouldn't have mentioned it. I didn't know about this order, but it's all part of the same pattern. Go see Nikki. I've used up my five minutes."

"Miles, what the hell were you . . ."

"Nikki can tell you."

The preacher went into the chickenhouse, letting the screen door slam shut behind him. Jeff hesitated, then walked to the house and knocked. Trouble was like a shadow. He couldn't catch hold of it to grapple with it, but it was there. He felt much the way Miles did. All he could do was to watch it develop.

Mrs. Rebus opened the door, smiling when she saw who it was. She was a delicate woman who hadn't been well since she'd come to Starbuck. The altitude, the doctor said, but Jeff wondered if it was due to the demands made on a preacher's wife. In any case, she was heavy now with her first child, and in spite of the inconvenience, she was in better health than when she had first come to the mesa.

"Come on in, Jeff," Mrs. Rebus said. "I don't know what's the matter with that Miles, keeping you out there like that."

"He had trouble keeping me." Jeff grinned at her. "I can talk to him any day."

"Sure you can," Mrs. Rebus said. "Now you get into the parlor and kiss Nikki like you meant it."

He walked through the kitchen and the front room, wondering what Mrs. Rebus meant. He parted the velvet portieres that separated the parlor from the front room, and then he understood, for Nikki had been crying. The instant she saw him, she jumped up and ran to him. "I thought you were never going to get here," she said.

He took her into his arms and held her hard against him, then she lifted her face to his and kissed him. He felt her tremble in his arms as if she were chilled. In a week she would be eighteen. In almost every way she was a mature woman. He had never seen her cry before; he had never even known her to be upset except when they had talked about getting married in the spring and decided there was no use to even try to get Ben Shortt's permission.

She tipped her head back, her dark eyes

21

searching his gray ones. She whispered, "Let's go to Placerville and catch the train. We'll lie about my age and get married tomorrow in Montrose."

He shook his head, not understanding. They had decided to wait until she was eighteen rather than have any trouble with Shortt. Jeff saw no reason to change their plans now.

"I'd like to," he said, "but I think we'd better wait."

"Please, Jeff."

He shook his head again, and led her to the leather couch where she had been sitting. He dropped down beside her and took her hand. "What's happened?"

She looked past him, her eyes fastened on the big black piano on the other side of the room that Miles Rebus had brought when he came to Starbuck, and yet, watching her, Jeff had the feeling she wasn't seeing the piano at all.

"You're right, Jeff," she said. "I'm wrong. I'm always wanting to jump off some high place and break my neck, but you think things out and make the right decisions."

"Did Ben hurt you? Did he try to whip you or something?"

"Whip me?" She brought her gaze to his face as if wondering whether he was serious

22

or not. "He wouldn't do that."

Nikki rose and walked to the window, restless and miserable and troubled by something that had happened. Jeff remained on the couch, sensing that for the moment at least she didn't want to talk.

He thought about how it had been with Nikki and Ben Shortt. He'd had two children, Sadie who had married a neighbor named Steve Lawrence and had died last year. She'd been childless. Shortt's son Bert had run away with an actress and had married her.

Bert had followed his wife from one mining camp to another, willing for her to make a living. Nikki had been too much trouble, her parents moving around as they did, so they had put her in a boarding school.

Four years ago Nikki's father and mother had been killed in a train wreck. Shortt didn't know he had a granddaughter until Nikki wrote to him after her parents' death. He went to Denver and brought her home. He loved her. Jeff didn't doubt that, but it was a selfish, possessive love that was worse than no love at all.

She turned to Jeff, her hands clenched at her sides. "Sometimes I think I hate Grandpa. The minute he hears we're married, he'll set out to ruin you."

"He can't hurt us, Nikki," Jeff said.

She dug into a pocket and finding a handkerchief, wiped her nose. "He'll try, Jeff. Miles says he's possessed by the devil. I'm not afraid of what he'll do to us, but I'm afraid of what he'll do to you. He'll try to make you share the crimes he commits. Don't go to Wineglass tomorrow. Send word that you're sick. Or broke your leg. Anything. Just stay away."

"I've got to go," he said. "I won't try to make you understand why. I guess there are lots of times during people's married lives when the husband has to do things which seem foolish to his wife."

She came back to the couch and sat down beside him. In Jeff's eyes she was a beautiful girl, and that, he told himself, was the way it should be. Her hair was so black it was almost blue. She had a pointed chin and dimples in her cheeks when she smiled, but there were no dimples now. She kept chewing her lower lip, looking at him and then turning her eyes away.

He said gently, "Nikki, you haven't told me what upset you?"

"Nikki." She repeated her name as if she hadn't heard what he said. "It's a silly name. Daddy gave it to me. He couldn't let me have a common name like Mary or Jane."

But he refused to be diverted. He said, "You've got to tell me."

"I don't know," she said. "Not exactly. He keeps talking about Tom Barren and Floyd Deems and the rest. He says they're rustlers and they're stealing him blind and he's going to stop it, even if he has to hang them. They're your friends, Jeff. Some of them, anyway. You can't get into a thing like that. You just can't."

"I won't," he promised, "but I've still got to go tomorrow. There's going to be a day when somebody stands up to Ben. Maybe I'll be the one and maybe tomorrow will be the day." He slipped an arm around her waist and brought her slender body against his, one hand over a breast. "Let's talk about us."

But it wasn't any good. Not today. He rose and looked down at her. He said, "I love you, Nikki. If you forget everything else, remember that."

"I'll remember," she said. "It's one thing I like to remember."

This wasn't the gay and lively girl who was Nikki Shortt. There was something she hadn't told him, he thought, but he wouldn't press her now.

He left then, thinking that Mrs. Rebus would do more for her than he could. But during the long ride home he was unable to forget the expression of sheer misery he had seen in her dark eyes.

CHAPTER III

Red Mesa was a long tableland running from the foothills of the San Juan Mountains on the east to the broken country beyond Deer Creek to the west. A series of ridges to the south finally lifted toward a single, perfect peak known as The Lookout. On the north the canyon of the San Miguel was a trench 500 to nearly 1,000 feet deep, the south wall holding only an occasional break by which a man could reach the river from the rim. In many ways Red Mesa was cow heaven, with good grass and good water, and summer graze neighboring the mesa on both the north and the south.

The Rafter A buildings were less than a quarter of a mile from the San Miguel Canyon. By crow flight they were six miles north of Starbuck. The road which Jeff Ardell followed after he left town was almost as direct as a crow would fly, curling now and then as it dropped into an arroyo and angled up the opposite slope. The rest of the time it lined out straight north through the sagebrush and grass and patches of greasewood.

Jeff passed the Wineglass buildings a mile north of Starbuck. They lay off the road fifty yards to the east, a two-story white house, a sprawling barn, a number of outbuildings, and a maze of corrals. Jeff glanced in that direction once and then looked straight ahead, his thoughts turning sour.

Ben Shortt had always been difficult, arrogant, and self-centered, but suddenly he had become worse, so much worse that he was unbearable. No, not suddenly. Jeff realized that immediately. The change had been gradual, going back four years to the time Shortt had brought Nikki to Wineglass. Not long after that he had bought a controlling interest in the bank in Starbuck. A few months later Matthew Ardell had been crippled. These three things had happened within a year, and it was in that year that Shortt had changed.

Or had he changed? Jeff considered the question as he rode, the shadow of horse and rider lengthening on the ground to his right. Maybe a man never really changed, maybe it was a simple case of a brake being applied to his greed and love of power, a

28

brake which had been removed when Matthew Ardell was limited to a wheel chair.

Jeff mentally added up the number of small outfits which had been absorbed by Wineglass. He could think of eight immediately. Some of the ranchers had stayed on the mesa and gone to work for Wineglass. Others had left the country. In no case had Shortt used force. He had either bought the ranches outright, or had used the bank to cut off their credit and force them to sell.

Now there were just the Big Four. How soon would it be the Big Three, with the Rafter A added to Wineglass?

It was time for supper when Jeff got home. He unsaddled, remembering the first time he had seen the mesa when he was no more than six, his father having brought a small herd over the mountains from the San Luis Valley. His mother had driven the wagon and Jeff had perched on the seat beside her.

The mesa was part of the Ute Reservation at the time. The Indians were to be moved out of Colorado to Utah, but some small bands were still here and Matthew had been warned against coming. He was a law-abiding man, and he knew he was trespassing, but it had seemed a fine line between what was legal and what wasn't, so he had refused to obey the warning.

Unfortunately, a small band of Ute braves saw him, and told him that if he wanted grass, he could have it. They made him get off his horse, go down on his hands and knees, and eat grass. Matthew Ardell never carried a revolver. He had a Winchester in the wagon, but he didn't try to use it. He obeyed the Utes, eating grass while the Indians rolled on the ground and laughed.

To some Matthew's conduct may have seemed cowardly, but when Jeff was older, he understood. If Matthew had resisted, he and his wife and son would have been killed. The proof of his courage was the fact that the Utes told him to get off the mesa and stay off or they'd kill him, but a week later he was back, this time alone.

Being the first on the mesa, he had his pick of locations. He had settled here because of the spring and the sprawling cottonwoods, he had built a cabin, and then, being sure the Indians were gone and there was no more danger, he had gone after his wife and Jeff.

Jeff realized that his father had many qualities which were admirable. For one thing, he had been satisfied with this corner of the mesa and his share of summer range on the Uncompahgre Plateau to the north. He gradually improved the property, replacing the cabin with a five-room house, fencing his pastures and hay meadows, and building a reservoir so that he always had water even in the dry years. But for some reason he and Jeff had never really understood each other.

Jeff thought about this as he turned his horse into the pasture, and walking to the log trough, took a drink from the pipe. He straightened and looked westward at the La Sal Mountains while he rolled a cigarette. The sun was almost down, the La Sals clothed by deepening shadows while above the peaks the sky burned with the scarlet brilliance of the sunset. He stood there until he finished his cigarette, thinking of his father and asking himself why they had never been closer than they were.

They were different. Matthew who hated violence had never understood why Jeff got into fights, why he liked to break wild horses, why he loved to go hunting with Lacey Dunbar and come back with nothing but the knowledge he'd had a hell of a good time.

On the other hand, as Jeff got older, he couldn't understand why Matthew dabbled in politics and stuck his nose into other people's business in the interest of peace. Most of all, he couldn't understand why people listened to Matthew, but the fact was they had.

Time after time Matthew had persuaded men to come to an agreement when it seemed that bloodshed was inevitable. Jeff didn't doubt that if his father could get on a horse and go to Wineglass, he would find a way to persuade Ben Shortt to let Tom Barren and Floyd Deems and the rest of them alone.

Jeff tossed his cigarette stub away, stepped on it, and walked through the dust of the yard to the house that was cool with the shadow of the cottonwoods upon it. Matthew was on the front porch in his wheel chair. He had never been a big man, but somehow he had contrived to give the illusion of bigness. Now he couldn't. He was a broken man, his face thin and lined, his hands all bones and knuckles. He said he couldn't live the year out and Jeff was inclined to believe it, but still Matthew retained his cheerfulness and he never, to Jeff's knowledge, complained about his condition.

Jeff asked, "How are you, Dad?"

"Fine." Matthew nodded and smiled. "Been a hot day, hasn't it?"

"Like an oven," Jeff agreed, and was silent. That was the way it usually went, an exchange of amenities and then a dead silence. Jeff knew he should talk to his father about Ben Shortt and ask him what he would do if he were Jeff, but it wouldn't do any good. Even if he knew what Matthew would do, he still wouldn't have an answer to his problem. He had the Ardell name, but he didn't have Matthew's talent for keeping men like Ben Shortt in line.

Jeff said, "I'll wash up. I guess supper's about ready."

"Ought to be," Matthew agreed.

Jeff went into the house. He sailed his hat into the corner and walked to the kitchen where his mother was taking a roast out of the oven. "I'm hungry, Ma," he said. "What have you got?"

"Plenty." She smiled at him, her face red with the heat. "Do you think there will ever be a time when a woman can cook a meal on anything besides a hot stove?"

He laughed as he pumped a basin of water. "Of course not," he said, and thought that was like his mother. She was always having crazy ideas. She even believed in dreams and ghosts. "What do you think would work — sunshine?"

"Maybe," she said. "The sun's hot, isn't it?"

"It's hot," he agreed. "You could grow

33

wings and fly up to the sun with your grub and wait till it cooks."

"Oh, wash up and quit making fun of me," she said in a cranky voice. "Fetch your pa in."

He grinned as he washed his face and hands. He shouldn't josh her that way. If a woman wasn't practical by the time she was forty, the chances were she never would be.

He combed his hair, and turning, stood looking at his mother. She had the appearance of a young woman, with no sign of gray in her chestnut hair, no wrinkles in her face, no slump to her shoulders. When he thought of other ranch women, he wondered how she had escaped the ravages of age.

Maybe she had retained her youth because Matthew had made her happy. She was married when she was sixteen. She'd had Jeff when she was seventeen, and if she had any regret about her married life, it was because she had been unable to give Matthew another son.

"You're mighty pert tonight," Jeff said. "You're getting younger instead of older."

"Won't work," she said tartly. "I don't know how you guessed I had a custard pie in the pantry, but you're not getting a second helping."

"I smelled it," he said, and going back to

the front porch, wheeled Matthew into the kitchen.

He sat down and his mother took the chair across from him. Matthew said the blessing, his skinny hands folded in front of him, his head bowed. As they ate, the thought occurred to Jeff that both his father and mother would make Nikki welcome, that they were not like Ben Shortt who was jealous and afraid he would lose Nikki's love. Just as everything Shortt did showed that he was basically selfish, so everything Matthew and Nancy Ardell did showed they were unselfish. Too much so, Jeff thought with some resentment.

If Matthew had thought more of his own interest, the Rafter A would be a far bigger spread than it was. Three men ran the outfit, Jeff and the two cowboys who were with the cattle on the Uncompahgre Plateau. By hiring Lacey Dunbar at roundup, and Miles Rebus to help with the haying, the Rafter A was well cared for.

When he finished, Jeff leaned back and rolled a cigarette. He said, "Nikki and me'll be getting married in a week."

"You've told her it will be here, haven't you?" Nancy asked.

"No. We'll get married in Miles's house. I don't want Ben making trouble here."

Nancy sighed. "Oh, I hate that man." She glanced at Matthew, then brought her gaze back to Jeff. "We want it to be here. It just wouldn't be right for us not to see our son married."

"I'll put Dad in the wagon and take him to town," Jeff said. "He can stand that much riding since it's a special occasion."

Matthew nodded. "You and Nikki do it the way you want to. But you're overestimating Ben. His bark's worse than his bite."

"Oh, you think the best of everybody," Nancy said. "Jeff, Tom was here this afternoon. He told us about the order Ben gave them. Matthew doesn't think it's serious, but I do."

"It's serious, all right," Jeff said. "Ben wants me to come to Wineglass tomorrow. Dolan and Lawrence will be there."

"The Big 4." Matthew shook his head. "I suppose he's got some scheme up his sleeve."

Jeff nodded. "He just wants us to tell him to go ahead with something he's already done, but I'm not going to. Dolan and Lawrence probably will, and then it'll be the Big 3."

"He won't do anything to us," Matthew said. "I remember when he first showed up on the mesa. It was several years after we

36

came. He almost got snowed in when he brought his herd across the mountains and he lost quite a few head. We had the daddy of all the bad winters I ever saw and he lost some more."

Nancy snorted in disgust. "That shows what he is. He'd have been wiped out if you hadn't given him hay. Then after the snow went off, the grass was so slow you almost lost your herd."

"I cut it pretty fine," Matthew admitted. "Anyhow, Ben knows I did him a favor. He won't hurt us."

"Well, I'm not so sure about that." Nancy turned to Jeff. "Tom wants us to sell out and throw in with him."

"I know," Jeff said, irritated because Tom Barren had insisted on pressing his proposition. "He had his answer."

"I told him the same," Matthew said. "This is a good outfit. In time it will be yours. We won't sell to Ben Shortt."

"And we won't throw in with Tom Barren," Jeff said.

"Correct," Matthew said.

Nancy began clearing the dishes, rattling them with unnecessary vigor. Matthew said gently, "Don't get your back up. Tom's a friend of ours, but that doesn't make him a desirable partner."

"All right," Nancy said. "So we'll sit here and let Ben Shortt shoot us in bed some night."

"Where did you ever get an idea like that?" Matthew asked.

"Get some wood for me, Jeff," Nancy said.

When he came in an hour later, he found that Matthew had gone to bed. Nancy was sitting on the front porch, the last color fading over the La Sals. She said, "It's nice out here, Jeff. I couldn't stand it in the house. I got so hot cooking supper."

He dropped down beside her. She went on, "It will be nice to have a woman to talk to. I get tired of just seeing men and cooking for men and hearing men talk."

"It'll be nice for me to have her here," Jeff said.

"It's the only way we'll ever have a daughter." She took a deep breath, then added, "I just wish Matthew would complain once in a while."

Jeff was surprised. It was the first time he had ever heard her be the least critical of his father.

CHAPTER IV

Jeff reached Wineglass Sunday afternoon shortly before two, which was the hour Ben Shortt had set for the meeting. The Wineglass buildings always gave Jeff the impression that here was a practical ranch, planned for utility. Shortt had picked a site atop a slight elevation in the very center of the mesa, the houses of Starbuck visible to the south. The rim of ridges and hills surrounding Wineglass range was punctuated on the east by the granite peaks of the San Juans and by the La Sals to the west.

Everything about Wineglass was big: the house, the barns, even the slab sheds, but the first thing which always struck Jeff when he came here was the complete absence of a woman's touch, no flowers, not even a tree. Here it was, set up on a ridge so that it could be seen for miles away, subject to every wind that blew across the mesa and without shade so it was hammered by the sun all summer.

It was like Shortt, Jeff thought, to bring Nikki here and tell her it was her home, but refuse her the right to beautify it. She had often complained about it to Jeff, how Shortt had told her it was a man's ranch and that it was going to remain that way.

Shortt grudgingly did give Nikki permission to do what she wanted to with her upstairs room, and as Jeff dismounted, he noticed the white curtains at her window. Apparently Shortt thought any hint of femininity was a mark of weakness, something he could not permit. That, to Jeff's way of thinking, was a sign of weakness itself.

Jeff tied, noting that Steve Lawrence's and Hank Dolan's horses were at the hitch rail. He was a few minutes early, but they had come even earlier, so they would have time to talk over what to do if Jeff refused to go along with whatever scheme Shortt was planning to propose.

Nikki opened the door before he knocked. She was pale, and from the swollen appearance of her eyes, he knew that she had been crying. He started to ask what the trouble was, but before he could say anything, she stood up on her tiptoes and kissed him.

"They're in his office," she whispered. "If

you have to make a run for it, go out through the window. None of the crew is here except the cook and Slim Tarrant. Slim's in the bunkhouse, so you'll have to watch out for him."

He stared at her in amazement. "Nikki, what . . ."

She put a hand over his mouth. "I didn't want you to come. Remember? Now listen. They're all wearing guns, but Tarrant's the one to look out for. Go on in and be careful."

Still he stood there, staring at her, too dumbfounded to make any sense out of what she was saying. Suddenly he wondered if Shortt had brought him here to murder him. The thought seemed ridiculous and he immediately dismissed it.

Then another idea came to him that was far more alarming. He demanded, "Are you in any kind of danger?"

"Of course not."

"There's something wrong," he said doggedly. "I want to know what it is."

"Nothing's wrong yet," she said, "but I know Grandpa and I know you. I should have told you yesterday. I don't know why I . . ."

The hall door opened and Ben Shortt said in his booming voice, "I thought I saw you

41

ride up, Jeff. Come on and we'll get started."
Jeff hesitated, his eyes still on Nikki, and
Shortt demanded, "What are you keeping
him out here for?"

"I wasn't," she said as she turned away. "I
just let him in."

"Come on, Jeff," Shortt said, paying no
more attention to Nikki as she walked down
the hall and disappeared.

"Sure, Ben," Jeff said, and followed Shortt
into the front room.

Shortt paused, his blue eyes studying Jeff.
He was a huge man, towering a good four
inches above Jeff who was over six feet. His
face might have been carved out of granite,
cold and arrogant, with a Roman nose and
fat lips and full jowls.

His skin had been burned to a dark brown
by long exposure to wind and sun; his eyes
were surrounded by a network of crow's
feet, and he continually squinted as many
men did who spent nearly all of their waking hours in the harsh light of the Colorado
high country. For a man of his age he was
surprisingly unmarked by the years. Except
for liver spots on the backs of his hands and
his white hair and white mustache which he
kept carefully trimmed, he showed no visible signs of being seventy years old.

"How's Matthew?" Shortt asked.

"Good," Jeff said. "As good as can be expected."

"I haven't seen him for a long time," Shortt said. "Been aiming to ride over and visit a spell, but never seem to get at it."

He was lying. He hadn't been to see Matthew since his accident, and Jeff was convinced he didn't want to see him, but there was no point in saying it. He'd play along until Shortt showed his hand.

"Dad would like to see you, Ben," Jeff said. "Better make it soon. He keeps saying he won't live the year out."

"Sorry to hear that." Shortt took two steps toward his office, then turned back. "Jeff, what was Nikki telling you?"

"Nothing," Jeff lied. "She must have been in the back of the house and didn't hear me knock at first."

Shortt shook his head. "I sure don't savvy that girl. She's got everything I can give her, but she ain't satisfied."

He turned again and this time went on into his office, closing the door behind Jeff. He motioned to a chair and sat down behind his cluttered desk. Jeff spoke to Lawrence, then Dolan, and both nodded warily, embarrassed and unsure of themselves.

Lawrence was a small, mousey man who

43

had married Shortt's daughter Sadie. He was nearly fifty and looked older. He owned Triangle on the southwest corner of Red Mesa, a bigger outfit than the Rafter A but smaller than Wineglass.

Sadie had died the year before, but the relationship between Shortt and Lawrence was still that of father-in-law to dutiful son-in-law, with Lawrence jumping every time Shortt waggled a finger at him. That was the behavior expected from his relatives, and was probably the reason Shortt didn't understand Nikki who had inherited much of her father's rebellious spirit.

Hank Dolan's outfit, the HD, was the size of Triangle and occupied the southeastern corner of the mesa. He was thirty-five, a thin, dyspeptic man who had an attractive wife and worried about her. His ranch was heavily mortgaged to the bank, giving Shortt a club he used to call the turn on Dolan.

Why Shortt had permitted Dolan to remain when he had closed out other ranchers in the last three years was a question. There was gossip about Shortt and Dolan's wife and perhaps Dolan closed his eyes to what was going on, knowing that if he objected, he'd lose everything he had.

Shortt took a cigar from a box, shoved it

at Jeff who shook his head, then at Dolan and Lawrence who helped themselves. Their chairs were next to the windows, Jeff's was against the east wall, and Shortt's faced the windows. If Nikki's hunch was right, he couldn't possibly hold the three of them under his gun.

Shortt bit off the end of his cigar, lighted it, then squinted at Jeff through the smoke. "How big a loss did you have last winter?"

" 'Bout three percent," Jeff said.

"Three percent." Shortt repeated the words as if he doubted the truth of them. "You sure?"

"I'm sure."

"Steve?"

"About ten."

Shortt made a sound of satisfaction. "Hank?"

"Under ten," Dolan said.

"Well boys, Wineglass lost more'n ten percent." Shortt leaned back in his swivel chair. "It's easy enough to see what happened. The God-damned rustlers are stealing me'n Steve blind.

"Steve's close to Deems and Barren and the rest of 'em on Deer same as me. Hank's got the other corner of the mesa, so his stock would be harder to get across the mesa and into Utah. Jeff's a friend of that

45

bunch, so they're letting him alone."

This was about what Jeff had expected. He didn't believe Wineglass and Triangle had lost ten percent, but there was no way he could prove it. Calling Shortt and Lawrence liars wouldn't do any good, so he tackled it from another angle.

He reached for tobacco and paper, saying, "Ben, you're wrong on one thing. Those men aren't my friends, not good enough friends to leave my stock alone if they're in the rustling business. Dunbar maybe, but none of the others."

Shortt chewed on his cigar, glaring at Jeff. "You trying to say I ain't losing cattle?"

Jeff shrugged. "I don't think the boys on Deer Creek are rustlers. That's what I'm trying to say. But it might be some outfit operating from the other side of the line."

Shortt slammed forward in his chair. "You'n me could ride over there to Deer Creek today and find a Wineglass hide in Tom Barren's backyard. Or we'll find a hide with the brand cut out."

"Maybe," Jeff agreed, "but what does Steve eat? And Hank?" He leveled a forefinger at Shortt. "You, too. Was there ever a day when we didn't have that piddling kind of stealing going on?"

"Piddlin'?" Shortt bellowed. "My God,

boy, do you call ten percent of my herd piddlin'?"

"No, but we've got to have proof that the
Deer Creek men are working on that big a
scale. It's not eating two or three steers a
winter which I figure is all they've done."

Dolan nodded agreement. "That's the way
I call it, Ben. We'd better hire a range detective and get some proof."

Shortt didn't like the opposition he was
getting and showed it. He said harshly, "If
they've butchered one of my steers, they're
rustlers and we'll hang 'em."

"No," Jeff said. "If we did, we'd have to
hang ourselves because I claim it's something we all do or have done. You've called
these men rustlers and ordered them to sell
and get out. If you've got proof of what you
say they are, let's have it."

Dolan unexpectedly nodded agreement to
this. "Yeah, I'd like to see it, Ben. I sure as
hell don't favor hanging a man like Tom
Barren till I know he's done more'n eat one
of my steers."

Shortt's ire was steadily rising, but he kept
his temper under control. "Steve, what do
you say?"

Lawrence hesitated, his face turning red.
"I figger we've got to clean 'em out, Ben,"
he said finally.

47

" 'Bout time one of you said that. Jeff, you and Hank are a pair of chicken-livered numbskulls. Now I figgered on you boys backing my play. The last time I went to Denver I hired a range detective. He'll be in Starbuck tomorrow. Or Tuesday at the latest."

"Well then," Lawrence said, "what are we arguing about?"

"I wanted to be sure the Big 4 is going to hang together," Shortt said. "We know we can't get the sheriff to come here. He won't even send a deputy to this end of the county, so it's up to us to do the job ourselves. I want you to help pay the detective. If the cost is too steep, I'll foot half the bill. The three of you divide the other half. That's fair, ain't it?"

Fair enough, Jeff thought. Too fair. There was a joker somewhere in the deck. He had a hunch Nikki knew what it was and hadn't wanted to tell him, but from the way Dolan and Lawrence had talked and acted, he didn't think either of them knew what it was.

One thing was clear. Shortt wanted all of them to share the responsibility for what he had already done. What the detective would do, too. The money, then, was not the important point.

Suddenly Jeff remembered what Tom Barren had said. Shortt wanted the Ardell name to be behind whatever he did, the name Matthew Ardell had made mean something. It would give an aura of respectability to any crime Shortt committed.

The silence ran on for a few seconds. Finally Steve Lawrence nodded. "Looks plenty fair to me, Ben."

Silence again, then Dolan said, "I guess it is, Ben. Only thing is I ain't sure we'd get any cooperation from the sheriff's office if we showed him enough evidence to choke on."

Shortt chewed on his cigar, then took it out of his mouth. "I'll see we get cooperation. What about you, Jeff?"

His tone was definitely questioning. Jeff said slowly, "Ben, you hired this bucko without asking us. Strikes me we should have had our say about hiring a man who'll nose around here and maybe kick up a lot of dust."

"I got the best man in the business," Shortt said harshly.

"Who did you hire?" Jeff asked.

Shortt hesitated just a moment, but it was long enough to reveal the uncertainty that was in him. Maybe he knew he had done the wrong thing and now was bound to bull it through.

"Sam Marks," he said.

A pulse began pounding in Jeff's temples. A lot of things were clear, so clear that suddenly Jeff was scared. In a quick flash of insight, he knew exactly what Nikki had meant when she said he might have to make a run for it.

For a time there was no sound but the labored breathing of all four men in the room, then Dolan said, "My God, Ben, he ain't a detective. He's a killer. We all know his reputation."

"I don't give a damn about his reputation," Shortt snapped. "I want a man who will get results. Marks will."

Jeff rose, his gun in his hand. He pointed it at Shortt. He said, "Ben, you've done some no-good things, but this is the worst. That's why you want us to hang together, and that's just about what we'd all do if we back you in this scheme."

"Put that gun down," Shortt snarled. "You gone loco?"

"No, I just want you to get this straight. I'll have no part of your deal. I'll tell Lacey Dunbar and the rest about Sam Marks. We'll run him down and kill him. He's a mad dog and you know it."

Shortt's eyes were pinned on the gun in

Jeff's hand. He bellowed, "Steve! Hank! Smoke this bastard down. We can't let him leave here and ruin everything."

"I aim to," Jeff said. "You boys drop your gun belts and get over here against the wall. Make a wrong move and Ben gets it right in the brisket."

"Here's mine," Dolan said. "I ain't backing Ben's deal this time."

Dolan dropped his gun belt and moved to stand behind Shortt. Lawrence hesitated, torn between his desire to please Shortt and his certain knowledge that if he pulled his gun, he'd force Jeff to shoot Shortt.

"Get over here," Jeff said. "I'm leaving and I don't want to be shot while I'm doing it."

Lawrence obeyed, dropping his gun belt beside Dolan's. It had been a gamble, but Jeff had judged both men correctly. Either one could have shot him while he was covering Shortt, but they had lacked either the courage or the conviction.

Shortt's gaze was on Jeff as if he couldn't believe he was actually being defied. Jeff said, "Let's have yours, Ben."

"I'll kill you, Ardell," Shortt said. "I'll hunt you down with every man I've got and I'll kill you."

"Your gun belt, Ben. You've run out of time."

Shortt rose and unbuckling his belt, tossed it on top of the other two. Jeff backed toward the windows, his gun still lined on Shortt. "If anybody comes out shooting, he'll get it. I hope it's you, Ben. It'll save a lot of trouble."

He picked up the gun belts and dropped them through an open window. Shortt was trembling, sweat making a bright shine on his face. He cursed Jeff, repeating his threat, but Jeff didn't listen. He went out through the window and ran for his horse.

Shortt yelled, "Get him, Slim. Shoot the son of a bitch."

So that was why Slim Tarrant was in the bunkhouse on a hot Sunday afternoon. Shortt had foreseen this possibility and had coppered all bets.

Jeff reached his horse just as Tarrant rushed out of the bunkhouse, his gun in his hand. Jeff threw a shot at him, so close it must have singed the side of his face. He wheeled and dived back through the door. Then Jeff was in the saddle.

Steve Lawrence reached through the window to get a gun from the belt Jeff had dropped. Jeff fired at him, the bullet smashing a window pane above Lawrence's head. He jerked back out of sight.

Jeff wheeled his horse and dug steel into

his sides. Tarrant opened up from the bunkhouse and Jeff fired back, then he was out of revolver range, bending low in the saddle, his horse running hard.

CHAPTER V

Paralysis gripped Ben Shortt as he watched Jeff go out through the window. Afterwards he had a vague memory of calling to Slim Tarrant to shoot Jeff. Then the shock of surprise was gone and he bellowed, "Don't let him get away."

Shortt wheeled to the door, flung it open, and ran into the front room to the antlers on the wall. He grabbed a rifle and turned to a front window that was open, not aware that Nikki was in the room. Shortt thumbed back the hammer and brought the stock to his shoulder, just as Jeff swung into the saddle. Shortt pulled the trigger. Nothing happened. Just the click of the hammer.

He tried to lever a shell into the chamber, his hands trembling. The magazine was empty. He threw the rifle down, not understanding it. He took down a second rifle, but it wasn't loaded, either.

He ran to the cherrywood sideboard and

yanked a drawer open. There should have been a box of .30–30 shells in it, but the box was gone. There should be a revolver here, a Colt .45, but it was gone, too. What the hell had happened?

He put a hand on his forehead. It was wet with sweat. His heart was pounding with great, hammering beats. He had a crazy feeling this was a nightmare. These things couldn't be happening. Both rifles empty. The shells and revolver gone.

He heard shots and ran to the window. Jeff's horse was stretching out in a dead run. He wasn't out of range yet, but he would be by the time Shortt found any ammunition. Tarrant had been firing from the bunkhouse, but apparently he hadn't hit Jeff or his horse.

"I wasn't going to let you murder him," Nikki said.

Shortt ran out of the house, not taking time to find out what the girl meant. Jeff had got away. Four of them were here to stop him. Slim Tarrant had been stationed in the bunkhouse for exactly that purpose, and still Jeff had got away.

All the crew was at the cow camp on the Uncompahgre Plateau or the one to the south on The Lookout except Slim Tarrant and Curly Jones. Well, three men were enough to catch the son of a bitch. If he'd gone home. If he headed for the broken country between here and the Utah line, twenty men couldn't find him.

Slim Tarrant stepped out of the bunkhouse, his gun in his hand. "I missed him, Ben. By God, I clean missed him."

Shortt was so furious he couldn't speak coherently. First he sputtered, then he cursed Tarrant, and finally demanded, "Why didn't you plug him? I told you . . ."

"I know what you told me," Tarrant interrupted. "I reckon I should have let him have it through the window, but I heard you yell and I went through the door, figuring he'd bust the breeze getting out of here. The trouble was he saw me and put a slug so close to my head I heard it talk to me as it went by. Next time he'd have got me, so I jumped back, then he was on his horse and moving."

Shortt stared at his foreman, wanting to curse him, wanting to reach out and slap him for being a damned fool. But Shortt was restrained by the thought that he couldn't afford to lose Tarrant with what was ahead. The foreman was too good a man.

"You've got to go after him," Shortt said. "Where's Curly?"

"In town sparking his girl."

"I told you . . ." Shortt stopped. No, he hadn't told Tarrant to keep Jones here. He hadn't thought it was necessary. "Get him. Won't take long to go to town and fetch him back. I'll go with you after Ardell. Three of us will be enough to handle him."

He wheeled and strode toward the house. Lawrence had come out through the window and picked up his gun belt. Dolan was inside the office buckling his around his waist. Shortt's was on the ground where Jeff had dropped it. Shortt bent over and picked it up, the red haze of fury still half blinding him.

"All you had to do was to go through that window and get your gun," Shortt shouted. "You should have plugged him before he got to his horse."

"I was a little slow," Lawrence admitted. "I started to, but he threw a shot at me that was too close to enjoy." He pointed to the bullet-smashed window pane. "I ducked back inside."

Shortt cursed him. "You and Tarrant! You could have got him in a cross-fire and one of you would have tagged him."

"Funny thing," Dolan said. "Looked to me like you had plenty of time to drill him from the other room if you wanted him

57

beefed. You've got two rifles in there. What were you doing?"

"They were empty," Shortt said curtly.

"So you don't keep 'em loaded."

Dolan was openly taunting him, something he had never done before. Shortt, staring at him through the open window, saw naked hate in the man's eyes. That was the way with men like Hank Dolan. Let Jeff Ardell get away with what he'd done and suddenly Hank was brave, too.

"Go fetch some of your men," Shortt said. "You, too, Steve. We've got to get Jeff."

"If you find him, you'll do it without my help." Dolan put a leg through the window and crawled out. "I've been on my knees long enough, Ben. When you bring in a killer like Sam Marks, you can foot the bill. All of it. Not me."

He walked toward his horse. Outraged, Shortt shouted at his back, "The bank will close you out in a week."

Dolan kept on until he reached his horse. He swung up, and then leaned forward, facing Shortt, his lips squeezed into a thin, ugly line. "You've kept me on my knees with that threat, but it won't work no more."

"You've got a wife and a family," Shortt said harshly. "Think you can support 'em by hiring out as a common cow hand?"

58

Dolan didn't move. Hatred stemming from the shame that had been in him for years was burning like a bright coal. He said, "Ben, it ain't no secret why I'm on the mesa when the others were pushed off. It don't make no difference anymore, so I'm telling you. You're a God-damned stud horse. If you ever come smelling around my wife again, I'll kill you."

He whirled his horse and galloped away. Shortt, staring at his back, knew that Dolan would do exactly as he had threatened. Well, there were other women. He didn't need Dolan. He didn't need the Ardells, either. This was the breakup of the Big 4, a pretense he had carefully nursed from the day Matthew Ardell had been injured. He had needed it then, but he'd grown to the place where he didn't need it now.

He turned, bringing his gaze to Steve Lawrence's face and looked at him as a man might look at a bug on the ground. He could squash it under his boot or let it live, depending on how he felt.

"How many men have you got at home?" Shortt asked.

"None but old Monty," Lawrence said. "They're at the cow camp."

"Go get 'em," Shortt said. "Bring back three of my boys. We'll try the Rafter A first.

If Jeff ain't there, we'll fine comb every ridge and arroyo between here and the Utah line. Might be we'll knock over Lacey Dunbar and Tom Barren while we're looking for Jeff."

"All right, Ben," Lawrence said, and walked to his horse.

Shortt went inside, remembering what Nikki had said about not letting him murder Jeff. It was plain enough what Nikki had done, but why? When he went into the front room, he saw a pile of shells on the table beside the missing revolver.

"I asked Jeff not to come today," Nikki said, standing beside the table, her head held high. "He wouldn't listen to me, so I unloaded the rifles and hid the box of shells and the revolver."

Shortt dropped into a chair. It seemed to him that all his plans had gone up in smoke in less than half an hour. In spite of himself, his thoughts turned to Bess Dolan. It had been a straight business proposition. She'd been willing, and Dolan had known all the time what was going on. Why should he get his neck bowed now? And why should Nikki give a damn about what happened to Jeff Ardell?

He rubbed his face with both hands, finding it hard to concentrate. The whole world had gone crazy and all because he had told Jeff he'd hired Sam Marks. Suddenly he felt every one of his seventy years. Unable to sit still, he rose and loaded the rifles and put them back on the antlers.

He thought of Matthew Ardell and how much he hated him, hated him because Matthew had done a favor for him the first winter he'd been on the mesa and in his subtle way had never let him forget it, hated him because people instinctively liked and listened to him and even sent him to the legislature, a miracle when Shortt remembered there weren't fifty votes in this end of the county and more than nine hundred in the mining camps in the east end.

He sat down again. For one of the few times in his life he was honest with himself and faced the truth. People didn't like him. They obeyed him because they feared him.

Even his own son had left home when he was a boy and had married a woman who was a disgrace to the Shortt name. His daughter had married Steve Lawrence because Shortt had made her give up the tinhorn gambler she thought she'd been in love with. Just Nikki left, and he wasn't sure she loved him.

He looked at her again, his mind going back and picking up what she had said. *She had told Jeff not to come.*

"I don't savvy," he said. "You haven't had a chance to tell Jeff anything."

"You might just as well know," she said. "I'm in love with him. We're going to get married the day I'm eighteen. I've been seeing him Saturday afternoons in Miles Rebus' house. We'd have told you, but we knew it would be the same as it was with Daddy."

Still he sat there, staring at her, hit so hard by what she had just said that it took a moment to fully comprehend it. Then he rose and walked to her, breathing hard. He slapped her across the side of the face, the blow turning her head and leaving the red imprint of his hand on her cheek.

"You ain't leaving Wineglass," he shouted. "You ain't marrying that bastard, neither. Understand?"

She held her eyes on him, hating him. She said, "You can't stop me. Do you think slapping me will keep me here?"

He raised his hand as if to hit her again, and lowered it. That had always been his way, with Nikki's father when he had been home, and with Sadie. His wife, too, when she'd been alive. They'd obeyed him, but they hadn't loved him. None of them. And Bess Dolan? She'd gone to bed with him because she loved her husband, not Ben Shortt.

All the bitterness and frustration of his whole life piled up and smashed the dam of his self-restraint. A wild, crazy rage took hold of him, and he put his hands on her throat, shouting, "I'll keep you from marrying him, all right." He might have killed her if Miles Rebus hadn't come in, and grabbing Shortt's hands, pulled them away from Nikki's throat.

Shortt wheeled on the preacher and tried to hit him, but Rebus ducked and coming up under the blow, hammered his stomach with a powerful punch that drove the breath out of Shortt and doubled him over. Rebus backed to the table and picked up a gun.

"I have never killed a man," Rebus said. "I never wanted to before." He shook his head, then asked, "What's the matter with you, Ben?"

Nikki had dropped down on the couch, a hand lifted to her throat. Shortt still labored for breath. Holding his stomach, he crossed to a chair and sat down.

"Put it down," Shortt said to Rebus. "I'm all right now." And to Nikki, "I'm sorry."

"Better come home with me, Nikki," Rebus said.

She shook her head. "I'll stay. He won't

do it again."

"She can't go with you," Shortt said. "I'm going to send her to Denver to school. She'll leave on the stage Tuesday."

"I won't go," she flared.

"You'll go all right. I've been neglecting you. I've thought about it ever since you came, but I wanted you with me." He scowled at Rebus, remembering the way he had come in. "You always walk into a house like this?"

"I knocked and no one answered," Rebus said. "Then I heard you yelling at her like a crazy man, so I came in."

Shortt was glad Rebus had, but he couldn't admit it. He asked, "What'd you want?"

"To see Nikki," Rebus said. "She wasn't in church this morning, so I called to see if she was sick." He turned to Nikki. "You can't stay here. He'd have killed you if I hadn't come in."

"I won't touch her again." Shortt pointed a big forefinger at Rebus. "I hold you responsible for this business with Ardell. Now get out of here. You'd best keep right on going off the mesa, too."

"You'd better go, Miles," Nikki said. "If you see Jeff, tell him I'm leaving on the stage Tuesday. Tell him I won't see him for a year."

Rebus said. "If anything happens to her, Ben, I'll hold you responsible. There are some things even Ben Shortt can't do."

Rebus walked out. Nikki didn't say anything, or even move from where she sat on the couch. Her throat was still red where Shortt had choked her. He sat staring at her, more ashamed of what he had done than he had ever been in his life.

Finally he rose, and sitting down beside her, put an arm around her, an awkward motion, for he had never before made the slightest gesture of affection.

"I'm sorry, Nikki," he said. "It was my temper. You're everything I've got. When I die, Wineglass and the bank goes to you. All I'm asking is that you stay in Denver a year, then if you still want Jeff, I won't stand in your way."

He saw that she didn't believe him. He rose. "You've got tomorrow to get ready."

He walked outside and waited by the corral gate until Slim Tarrant returned with Curly Jones. He said, "Go to the Rafter A and find Jeff Ardell. Kill him. I aimed to go with you, but something's come up that makes it impossible for me to leave."

Tarrant shook his head. "Murder ain't my . . ."

65

"It won't be murder," Shortt said. "Chances are when he sees you he'll try to kill you. If he does, I'll give a thousand dollars to whichever one of you gets him."

Curly Jones was a knot-headed man who had drifted in the fall before at roundup. He was on the dodge, Shortt judged, and looking ahead, decided he could use the man. Now Jones nodded eagerly. "I can use a thousand dollars, boss," he said.

Shortt watched them ride away, then he returned to the house. Nikki wasn't in sight. Shortt hesitated, knowing he would have to watch her or she'd walk out on him. But it was better to leave her alone now. She was probably upstairs in her room.

He went on into his office. Lifting a bottle from a desk drawer, he took a long drink. Then he thought of Matthew Ardell. He had to stay here to keep Nikki from leaving, then he wondered if that was the real reason. Or was he afraid to face even a crippled Matthew Ardell who had once done him a favor? He wasn't sure.

CHAPTER VI

When Jeff left Wineglass he expected to be pursued. Shortt could not afford to permit word of Sam Marks's coming to get out, so he had no choice. He had to come after Jeff.

The distance between Jeff and Wineglass stretched out to a mile, then two, but there was still no sign of pursuit. Suddenly the significance of what he had done struck Jeff. Sam Marks might not be needed. Shortt would claim Jeff was an outlaw, he'd call his men a posse, and by the time he finished hunting Jeff, he'd have cleared Deer Creek of every man and his family.

It would have been smarter, Jeff thought ruefully, to have agreed with Shortt and left Wineglass a member in good standing of the Big 4. Then he could have warned Dunbar and the others about Sam Marks. Now all he could do was to get word to them as fast as he could.

He rode directly west, and reaching the

edge of the mesa in early evening, dropped down into the narrow valley of Deer Creek. He hit it a quarter of a mile upstream from Red O'Toole's ranch. He swung right, thinking he would warn O'Toole and let him spread the word, but when he reached O'Toole's place, he found no one there.

He dismounted and pumped water into the trough for his horse, then put his hand over the snout to back the water up, and had a drink. For a time he stood staring at the log cabin, the pole corral, the slab shed, and the yard with its white-crusted spot in front of the door where Mrs. O'Toole threw her wash water.

A skinny milk cow and a wobbly calf stared curiously at Jeff from a pasture west of the buildings. A dozen Plymouth Rock hens with droopy combs dusted themselves in the yard between the cabin and the slab shed. A bony, white-and-tan hound that was sleeping in the shade of the shed got up, scratched languidly, and went back to sleep.

Red O'Toole's place was typical of all the little outfits along Deer Creek except Tom Barren's. They were a shiftless lot, these Johnny-come-latelies, Jeff thought, and he admitted grudgingly that Ben Shortt was at least partly right in calling them riffraff. Tom Barren was the only one who was making an honest effort to get the most out of his ranch.

Shortt had a right to be sore about them living off Wineglass beef. If, as he claimed, some of them were involved in a big scale rustling operation, he was justified in doing something about it since he couldn't get any cooperation from the sheriff. Then Jeff's mouth hardened. Regardless of the losses he suffered, Shortt was not justified in bringing in a killer like Sam Marks.

Jeff mounted and rode on out of the narrow valley, deciding that no harm would come to O'Toole or his neighbors tonight. He'd go on to Lacey Dunbar's place and lay it in his lap. He wasn't sure what he'd do after that. Maybe it would be better to get out of the country for a while.

For an hour he rode across innumerable arroyos and rocky ridges, a dry, barren country that was poor grazing land at best. Probably Floyd Deems and Red O'Toole and the rest were bitter with envy every time they looked at the fine grass on Red Mesa and compared it to these cedar-covered slopes where a cow could never get fat because she had to work too hard simply to keep alive.

Still, there was much these people could do. Deer Creek was a good-sized stream which ran all year. A few dirt dams would hold back enough water to irrigate every acre of tillable land along the creek. The men could raise gardens, but none of them did. A ditch along the west slope would enable them to put water on some of the bench land and triple their pastures. But these improvements required hard work, and none were willing to put out the effort except Tom Barren.

By the time Jeff climbed to the top of Tate Mesa where Lacey Dunbar lived, the sun was completely down. He followed a game trail through the dense scrub oak and service berry brush, climbing steadily, and by the time it was fully dark, he reached the narrow road which ran east and west between Dunbar's cabin and Tom Barren's ranch on Deer Creek. The moon rose, a great, yellow ball floating up into the sky above Red Mesa. Jeff was in the spruce now, so dense that the trees blotted out the moonlight, making it almost impossible to see the road. Farther on, the trees were scattered and he was able to make better time.

Now and then he crossed small parks, the moonlight so bright that it might have been day. The thought occurred to Jeff that once Sam Marks was here, it would be suicide to cross clearings like these. Marks was the kind who would hide in the edge of the timber and shoot a man out of his saddle.

He judged it was nearing midnight when he reached the clearing that held Dunbar's cabin, barn, and corral. He reined up in the fringe of the timber fifty yards from the cabin, calling, "Lacey."

It was never safe to ride in before calling out. Dunbar lived within a few miles of the Utah line, and it was common knowledge that outlaws bound for the safety of Robber's Roost crossed Tate Mesa because it was easier traveling than through the broken country to the north.

If there was anything to Shortt's claim that he was being robbed blind, the chances were that the stolen Wineglass cattle had been moved across Tate Mesa. In any case, Lacey Dunbar was the kind of hair-trigger man who shot first and asked questions later.

From where Jeff sat in his saddle he could not see the cabin clearly, for it was in a scattering of aspens, the alternating patches of shadow and moonlight making the cabin and yard appear weird and unreal. Jeff remained motionless as he heard Dunbar's door squeak open.

Silence, then, until Dunbar called, "Who is it?"

"Jeff."

"Oh, for God's sake," Dunbar yelled. "Come on in."

Jeff rode toward the cabin, calling, "I hollered to keep my head from getting blowed off. You'd be real sorry if you came out shooting and I got a slug between the eyes."

"So would you, son," Dunbar threw back, laughing. "Well, get down and I'll make some coffee. Here's a lantern. You know where to put your horse."

When Jeff walked into the cabin a few minutes later, Dunbar had built a fire and had put the coffeepot on the stove. He was slicing venison steaks when he heard Jeff come in. He said, "You pick the damnedest times to visit. You know, it's a wonder I didn't cut loose. I figured you was one of Shortt's men."

Jeff tossed his hat into a corner, and pouring water from a bucket into the washpan, sloshed water on his face. He dried, then hung up the towel. He was always amazed at Dunbar who lived alone because he liked being alone, who hated to go to town, who affected long hair and a beard, and when asked why he didn't get married, always said, "Hell, I'm a good housekeeper. What can a woman do I can't do for myself?" He was right about being a good housekeeper. Except for the rumpled blankets on the bunk, the room was immaculate.

Jeff sat down and rolled a smoke. Dunbar put the frying pan with the venison steaks on the front of the stove, the aspen wood crackling fiercely. He set the table, then brought out a plate of cold biscuits, a jar of syrup, and a dish of beans.

"You ain't going to eat alone, son," Dunbar said. "Just looking at your skinny face and watching you swallow your spit is enough to make me hungry. Now suppose you tell me why you got me out of bed in the middle of the night?"

Jeff told him what had happened. Dunbar scratched the side of his bearded face, scowling, but he didn't say anything until he brought the frying pan to the table and forked the steaks onto the plates. Then he set the pan on the back of the stove and motioned for Jeff to pull his chair up.

"Sam Marks," he said. "Well, Shortt's done it now."

Dunbar ate with gusto, and Jeff couldn't keep from asking, "Didn't you have any supper?"

"Hell yes, but that was four, five hours ago."

He produced a bottle of whisky, poured Jeff a drink, and took one himself. He got out his pipe and filled it, then, cuddling it

73

in his hand, stared at it.

"Funny how things get complicated," Dunbar said. "I don't want to be bothered by nobody, and I don't bother nobody. I trade a horse off once in a while, I work for you every spring and fall. I get drunk two, three times a year and have me a good fight just to get the bile out of my system. That's what I call a good life. Now tell me why Shortt wants to run me out of the country?"

"Why does he want to run anybody out?" Jeff asked.

Dunbar lighted his pipe. "I didn't say so in town yesterday because I was sore about getting Shortt's note. Red O'Toole rode up here to get me and said there was a meeting, so I went, but since then I've been thinking. You know, Shortt's right about their rustling. I ain't in it and I don't think Tom Barren is. What gravels me is that Shortt don't bother to find out who's doing it."

"Who is doing it?"

"Just about all of 'em but me'n Tom. They run the Wineglass cattle across this mesa. There's another outfit operating on the other side of the state line that takes 'em, works the brands over, then sells 'em in the San Juan mining camps. Now why should I get beefed just because Ben Shortt figures

I'm in the business?"

"No reason," Jeff said.

He wished Dunbar hadn't told him about the rustling. He hadn't believed it because he hadn't wanted to, and now it bothered him that Shortt actually had grounds to take the step he had. Still, no amount of stealing justified sending for Sam Marks.

"The old bastard'll sure be on your tail," Dunbar said. "You'll be a hunted man as long as Shortt can send anybody after you. Me, too. Marks will bushwhack two or three men and that will start every thieving son of a bitch there is on Deer Creek to running. They're a poor bunch, Jeff. Won't work. Marry their girls off when they're fourteen. Always trying to get into bed with some neighbor's wife and making the grade most of the time."

Dunbar shook his head. "To hell with 'em, son. Let's saddle up in the morning and ride out of here."

Jeff had thought about doing that very thing, but now, hearing it from Lacey Dunbar, it didn't sound right. He said, "I can't do it, Lacey. Anyhow, this is your home. You've got horses. You can't just ride off and leave them."

"Let Shortt have 'em. I've got a couple good animals in the corral. I'll take them."

He chewed on his pipe stem as he stared at Jeff, then said, "Now tell me why you can't pull out."

"I can't go off and leave my folks. And there's Nikki. I'm aiming to marry her in a week."

Dunbar groaned. "You're a genuwine, ring-tailed, unadulterated fool. I don't take Shortt for a brave man. But Slim Tarrant is, and that Curly Jones is a tough nut if I ever seen one. Now Shortt will have Sam Marks, too. You marry up with Nikki and Shortt will have you shot so fast you'll stink before you hit the ground."

"He'll try, all right," Jeff said, "but I'm not going to run." He was silent a moment, thinking of his father, then he added, "I guess the biggest reason is that Matthew Ardell is my dad. He never ran from anything and I'm not going to. I keep hearing how much he made the Ardell name mean. He did it without carrying a gun or even getting into a fight as far as I know. In my book he had a lot of guts. Well, I'm not going to make the Ardell name mean something different if I can help it."

Dunbar studied Jeff a moment, a smile behind his heavy mustache. "That's the trouble with having Matthew Ardell for your pa." He shrugged. "Well, let's clean up the dishes and roll in."

"What'll we do in the morning?"

"We'll pass the word. We figured out a scheme in town. You go see Red O'Toole and he'll build a fire on the rim above his house. When the boys downstream see the smoke, they'll come a-running. I'll pick up Tom Barren and Floyd Deems on the way down the creek if they haven't seen the smoke."

He cleared the table, then laughed. "Just one thing, son. Watch out that O'Toole woman don't get you to bed with her before the meeting's over. That and stealing from Ben Shortt is all they think about."

"Nothing to keep you from riding out," Jeff said.

"Not a thing," Dunbar agreed amiably, "but if you're going to die of bravery, I might as well go to hell with you. Well, we can sleep tonight. Maybe tomorrow. But after that any time you or me go through that door, we can expect a hunk of lead right in the brisket. I'm a good one for 'em to start on, and after what happened today, Shortt will double Marks's pay if he gets you."

Jeff nodded, realizing that was exactly what Ben Shortt would do.

CHAPTER VII

The crowd began gathering at O'Toole's place shortly before noon. Floyd Deems rode in about twelve, and Tom Barren, unable to see the smoke signal from where he lived, arrived with Lacey Dunbar an hour later.

These men would clean up to go to town, Jeff thought, but now they were in their work clothes, dirty and unshaven, and Jeff could not keep from thinking of what Lacey Dunbar had told him about them. The exception was Tom Barren who, even though he had been irrigating, was as neat and dapper as he had been when Jeff had talked to him in the Belle Union Saturday afternoon.

O'Toole's wife, who had the incredible name of Butterfly, put on a clean dress when she saw Jeff ride up, brushed her hair, and applied rouge liberally to both cheeks. O'Toole said blandly Jeff might just as well get acquainted with his wife while he climbed to the rim and started the signal fire, but Jeff wanted none of that.

O'Toole tried to quiz Jeff about why the meeting was being called, but Jeff refused to answer. He simply said he had found out what Ben Shortt aimed to do. Later in the morning when the others rode in, Jeff remained aloof. That seemed to be the way O'Toole's neighbors wanted it. Jeff didn't belong; he was still a nabob to them.

He'd had some sympathy with these men in the past because they were forbidden the grass on Red Mesa. They had howled about the injustice of Ben Shortt's edict, claiming it wasn't right for them to be forced onto hardscrabble range because they were late getting here. Jeff had had even more sympathy for them after knowing Shortt had ordered them to sell and get out, but now he had no sympathy whatever. Matthew Ardell had taught him that a man deserved nothing more than he was willing to work for, and of all the men on Deer Creek, only Tom Barren was willing to work.

Mrs. O'Toole made no offer to feed them. They stood around the slab shed talking until Dunbar arrived with Barren and Alton. Barren stepped out of the saddle at once, nodded to the men by the shed, then strode to where Jeff stood by himself and shook hands.

"So we're prime targets," Barren said grimly.

"Lacey told you?"

Barren nodded. "It's a hell of a note," he said in a low tone. "I've lived on Deer Creek twelve years and I've got a good little outfit. Now I'll lose it because Ben Shortt wants more range." He swung around, his usual poker face replaced by an expression of explosive anger. "Well, I'm damned if I'll let him have it. Let's get it over with. We've got to figure out something."

Jeff followed Barren to the shed. Barren said, "Jeff's got something to tell us, something mighty God-damned bad." He nodded at Jeff. "Tell them."

"Shortt sent for a range detective to get the deadwood on whoever is stealing Wineglass cattle," Jeff said. "If it was an ordinary detective who would make an honest effort to hunt up some evidence, there wouldn't be any trouble. That is, unless Shortt's right about you boys rustling Wineglass beef."

They looked away, refusing to meet his gaze. Even Barren was staring at the rim across the creek. Lacey Dunbar, standing away from the others at the corner of the shed, seemed amused by the entire performance. O'Toole ran a worn boot toe back and forth through the dust, then broke the silence with, "Well?"

"I had a fight with Shortt over it," Jeff said. "He hadn't asked the rest of us. He just went ahead and hired a range detective, expecting Lawrence, Dolan and me to foot part of the bill, but it wasn't the money he was after. My hunch is that what he wanted was our backing, which he'd have had if we'd paid our share of the detective's pay. I had to make a run for it when I left Wineglass. Slim Tarrant threw some lead at me. Shortt promised he'd send his boys after me, so I figured I'd hide out with some of you."

That startled them. They looked at him, more uneasy than ever. Lacey Dunbar laughed. "Speak up, Red. Floyd, how about you? Which one of you will hide Jeff?"

"I dunno that we're obligated to do that," O'Toole said. "We'd be fools to go looking for trouble."

"That's what we'd be doing," Floyd Deems said, "and it's too much to ask. We've all got wives except you and Tom. Most of us have children. If Shortt's gunning for Jeff and finds him in one of our homes, he'd wipe us out. We can't take no chances like that."

"Brave men," Dunbar said with biting contempt.

"You're single," Deems said. "Why don't you hide him?"

"I will," Dunbar said, "and be glad to do it."

"Well, what are you warnin' us about?" O'Toole demanded. "I'll put Ardell up if he wants a change of cookin' from what you give him, but I don't figure this is a very safe place for him."

"My place ain't safe, either," Dunbar said. "I don't know of any place around here that is going to be safe."

"I don't intend to move in with any of you," Jeff said. "I was curious about what you'd say. Now I've heard it, and I don't much care what happens to any of you except Lacey."

"You know you're welcome to stay with me," Barren said.

"I'll add you to Lacey," Jeff said. "The rest of you are a bunch of gutless wonders. Why don't you sell to Shortt and get out of the country?"

He walked to his horse. He had expected something from these men, and yet, knowing them, he realized he shouldn't have expected anything.

"Wait a minute," O'Toole shouted. "You

told me to get everybody together. I done it, and I say we've got a right to know who this yahoo is that Shortt hired."

"Sam Marks," Jeff said, and swung into his saddle.

"Marks," Deems said, visibly jolted.

"If some of you boys don't know who he is," Barren said, "I'll tell you. He raised hell in Wyoming with some little fellows that the nabobs wanted exterminated. That's what he is, an exterminator. He's worse than Tom Horn ever dreamed about being."

"He's the kind who'll hunker across the creek in them boulders," Dunbar said, "and some morning when Red comes through his front door, he'll get it between the eyes. You'll never know what hit you, son."

Somebody laughed, a hysterical sound more than one of humor. The man said, "Come night, Red, your wife'll miss you."

Jeff jerked his head at Dunbar. "Let's ride, Lacey."

"Hold on," Barren called. "We've got to decide on something. We're goners if we don't shoot Ben Shortt and burn his place out. Marks won't stay when he hears Shortt's dead. All he's interested in is his pay." Barren swung to face Jeff. "What about Lawrence and Dolan?"

"Lawrence will stick," Jeff said. "I don't

83

think Dolan will."

Barren turned back. "How about it, boys? Let's meet here after dark. Bring all the guns you've got. I'll go to town and get some dynamite. Be better than burning Wineglass."

"Good idea," Dunbar said.

Red O'Toole nodded reluctant agreement. "I reckon that's right."

But that was as far as it went. "I don't think we need to risk our lives fighting Wineglass," Deems said.

"Maybe it's just bluff," another said.

"Hell, we don't even know that what Ardell says is true," a third one said. "Let's wait and see if this Sam Marks shows up."

Jeff's immediate impulse was to get off his horse and beat the man until he apologized for calling him a liar. Then he shrugged and turned his horse upstream. What was the use? They weren't worth fighting; they weren't even worth saving.

Lacey Dunbar caught up with him, laughing silently behind his beard. "I told you, son," he said. "We had to tell 'em, but all you got out of it was getting called a liar. You should have busted his head."

"I thought of it," Jeff said, "but I decided I had better heads to bust."

"You have for a fact," Dunbar agreed.

84

"Well, you'n me and Tom could tackle Wineglass. Maybe Red. Ain't enough, is it?"

"No, not if Ben calls his crew in. I didn't like the sound of it anyhow, with Nikki there."

They rode in silence until Tom Barren caught up with them. He said harshly, "Four men with enough sand in their craw to do something. Out of that whole bunch, just four."

"I ain't staying around for Marks to plug," Dunbar said. "What are you going to do, Jeff? You can't go home."

"I can't yet," Jeff agreed. "It's Nikki I'm worried about. I've got to get her off Wineglass, but I don't know how to do it."

"Tom?" Dunbar asked.

Barren was staring straight ahead to where the walls of the canyon almost met, the creek narrowing at this point and becoming a fierce torrent for fifty yards. The trail that clung to a shelf along the west wall was barely wide enough for a horse. Barren couldn't be heard above the roar of the water, but when they reached Floyd Deems's hay meadows above the Narrows, he touched his horse up and pulled in beside Jeff and Dunbar.

"I've been thinking ever since I got that damned note about what I ought to do,"

Barren said, "but I still don't know. Gives a man a queer feeling in his belly when he knows he might not have more than another twelve hours to live."

"Get out," Dunbar said. "Like me."

"No," Barren said. "I won't give Ben Shortt that much satisfaction. I've worked too hard on this spread to turn it over to him." He pinned his gaze on Jeff's face. "Have you thought over my proposition?"

"You had my answer."

"Would it be different if I moved in with you?" Barren pressed. "The only chance we've got is to work together. Lacey's pulling out. That just leaves Red. I'd even take him in if it was necessary."

Dunbar laughed. "That'd mean taking his wife in, too."

"This is a question of staying alive," Barren said. "I'd put up with that bitch if I had to."

They were silent again, each busy with his own plans and his own troubles. Jeff couldn't get his mind off Nikki. If Shortt found out they were planning to get married, anything could happen. He probably knew by now. Nikki would find it hard to keep her feelings to herself after the trouble Sunday afternoon.

Presently they reached Barren's ranch

with its white frame house, log barn, tight fences and corrals. Jeff had been here several times and always found it looking the same, as if Barren took pride in his spread, a pride that was not evident anywhere else on Deer Creek. He had something to fight for, and that, Jeff thought, would very likely give Shortt sufficient reason to send Marks gunning for Tom Barren before he murdered anyone else.

Miles Rebus was waiting in front of Barren's house. As soon as they appeared around a bend in the creek, he spurred toward them. He reined up beside Jeff, telling him that Nikki was leaving the country on the Tuesday stage to go to school in Denver.

"Shortt and Nikki had a ruckus," Miles finished. "Nikki doesn't want to go, but looks like she'll have to."

"Hell, he figures she'll see somebody else she'll want if he gets her away from here," Jeff said, so furious he found it hard to say anything. "Well, she's not getting on that stage. I'll get her out of Shortt's house if I have to shoot the whole damned Wineglass crew."

"That ain't the way," Dunbar said. "Wait till tomorrow. We'll take her off the stage, then we'll hear old Ben howl."

"That'd be better, Jeff," Miles said. "If you go busting in on Wineglass, she'll get hurt and you'll get killed."

Jeff nodded, knowing they were right, but he wasn't sure he could stand the waiting for another twenty-four hours.

CHAPTER VIII

It was still early in the afternoon when Miles Rebus left Tom Barren's ranch to return to town, and Jeff and Lacey Dunbar turned west on the road that led to Tate Mesa. Barren told Dunbar that it was foolish to sleep in his cabin tonight, that Sam Marks would certainly come gunning for him because Ben Shortt knew Lacey Dunbar was a man who wouldn't scare. It was only natural that Shortt would order the murder of the man who had enough courage to fight back.

"Same applies to you," Dunbar retorted.

Barren knew that it was true. Now he sat on his front porch, thinking about it. The only other man on the creek with a spoonful of guts was Red O'Toole, and, after two murders, he'd cave.

Barren tried to get his mind off his physical danger. He thought about the work he had to do, and then he felt guilty because he wasn't working in one of his meadows.

Or hauling manure out of the corrals and sheds. He hated that job and managed to put it off to the last. But guilty or not, he would do no more work today. He wouldn't do any work until he was sure he was going to survive Ben Shortt's scheming.

He filled his pipe and smoked it thoughtfully, wondering if he could turn this situation to a profit for himself. He was not an honest man and he knew it, having no illusions about himself, but his dishonesty was not the stupid brand that cursed men like Deems and O'Toole and the rest of his neighbors.

Rustling was bound to get a man hanged sooner or later. If Ben Shortt had a brain in his skull, he'd have sent for a legitimate range detective to gather evidence, and then, without any fear of getting into trouble with the law, he could have hanged the bunch of them.

But sending for Sam Marks was something else. It had alienated Jeff Ardell and probably Hank Dolan, and it could end up with Ben Shortt being an outlaw himself. So, the way Barren saw it, bringing Sam Marks to Red Mesa was as foolish on one side as rustling Wineglass cattle was on the other, yet it was typical of the things Ben Shortt did.

Barren's dishonesty ran to other channels. He would steal Matthew Ardell's wife if he could, for he had been in love with her a long time. He would turn against his friends if he saw profit in it. He would even kill a man if it seemed necessary.

More than anything else, he wanted to retain his good name, even to add to it. He had often promised himself two things: Matthew Ardell's wife, and a name which was as respected as Matthew's had been before his accident.

By the time he finished his pipe, he had decided what he'd do. Tomorrow, with Sam Marks on the prowl, was another matter. He tightened the cinch, and stepping into the saddle, rode east until he topped Red Mesa, then angled northward toward the Rafter A.

He looked back once and smiled with satisfaction. In some respects he had done well in the twelve years he had been here. His small herd of purebred Shorthorns was the best in the country. His hay meadows, the dam he had built on Deer Creek, his buildings, the summer graze he claimed on Tate Mesa: all were things in which he could take justifiable pride. But they weren't enough.

When he came here he was not quite

twenty-eight. At that time he had set forty as the age when he'd be a man of wealth and respect. Now he was three months short of his fortieth birthday. He had less than $2,000 in the Starbuck bank. Not enough. Not nearly enough.

If Nancy Ardell were a widow, he was sure she would marry him, but Matthew might live for ten years and Tom Barren didn't have ten years to wait. Somehow he had to contrive to make her a widow, and that wasn't easy with a husband who was an invalid.

He had thought about this for months, but he had never arrived at what seemed a practical answer. That was one reason he wanted the Ardells to move in with him. If they were living in the same house, he could maneuver around in some manner so he'd be rid of Matthew and it would appear to be an accident.

He reached the Rafter A in late afternoon. Matthew was in his wheel chair on the front porch. He never left the ranch and he had few visitors. For that reason he was always glad to see Barren whose visits were at least breaks in what had become a dull life.

Matthew called to him to put his horse up and come in, that supper was almost ready. When he sat down on the porch a few minutes later, Nancy had come out of the kitchen for some fresh air.

Barren said, "Who comes oftener than me?"

"You can't come too often," Matthew said. "You know, Tom, I'm only forty-five, but lately I've been thinking like an old man. You know, living in the past, so I'm grateful for your visits."

"I'm glad to come," Barren said, his eyes on Nancy.

She was a fine-looking woman, he thought, unbelievably young appearing to be over forty. She was one of those rare women to whom age added a luster that had been missing when she was younger. As he remembered it, she was just about his age. She had no wrinkles except the tiny crow's feet around her eyes; he had never seen a gray hair in her head, and her blue eyes usually sparkled with the zest of merely being alive. Barren found this hard to understand, knowing she had been married to a man who had not been a husband to her for three years.

Tonight she seemed tired. Barren asked, "What's wrong, Nancy? You're upset about something."

"She's worried about Jeff," Matthew answered for her. "Last night a couple of

Shortt's men came here looking for him. He went to Wineglass in the afternoon, but he never got home."

Barren was silent a moment, then he said slowly, "That's why I rode over this afternoon." He paused, wanting Nancy to read his face, to sense his feeling for her. He thought she did, for he saw color rise in her cheeks and she looked away.

He never worried about what Matthew might think, for Matthew was the trusting kind who always wanted to see good in people. He would never think evil of his friend, Tom Barren, and under no circumstances would he distrust his wife.

"You saw Jeff?" Nancy asked in a strained tone.

"Just before I left home," Barren said. "He's with Lacey Dunbar."

"He's all right?" Nancy asked.

"Couldn't be better," Barren said heartily. "He can look out for himself if any man can. I guess you're mighty proud of him, the way he's taken over here and everything."

"I am," Matthew said. "More proud than I can tell you."

She said abruptly, "Supper's almost ready, Tom. Come in and wash up if you want to."

"I will," he said. "Thank you."

He waited until she was in the kitchen, then he said to Matthew in a low voice, "I didn't want her to know, but all of our trouble has come to a boil. The Wineglass men who were here yesterday would have killed Jeff if they'd found him. Ben Shortt is bringing Sam Marks into the country. That's why Jeff is on the dodge."

Matthew was startled, then he shook his head. "Ben is a greedy man, Tom. Something of a coward, too, I think. He's got a streak of meanness in him I never liked, but I always found him reasonable, once he got over his spell of cussing and ranting around. I can't think he's a murderer, though."

Barren expected this from Matthew. He said, "I've told you. You can think what you want to. But there's one thing you never figured out. Ben Shortt hates you. That makes him hate Jeff."

"Oh hell, Tom," Matthew said tolerantly. "Ben's got no reason to hate me."

"He's got plenty, being the kind of bastard he is," Barren said. "He's always wanted to be the big man in this country, but you were in his way. After you were laid up, you couldn't stop him, so he began expanding. He doesn't need our hardscrabble range, but he'll take it anyway. That's why he sent for Sam Marks."

"But there has been some rustling, I hear."

"Perhaps," Barren conceded, "but if he had just wanted to stop the rustling, he'd have sent for a different man than Marks. This way he'll get me and Lacey Dunbar, and Jeff if Marks can find him."

Barren rose and walked back to the kitchen where he washed at the sink and combed his hair. He had said more to Matthew than he intended to, but it was all right. In the end it might be the means of forcing Matthew and Nancy to come to him.

He was sure he had Ben Shortt figured correctly. Barren had one thing in common with the Wineglass owner — a sense that time was running out. How much more strongly would he feel if he were seventy instead of forty?

Shortt had undoubtedly looked back across the years, measuring his ambition against what he had actually accomplished, and then, acutely aware that he had only a little time left, had deliberately set out on the bloodsoaked path he would never have considered taking a few years ago.

When Barren turned from the mirror hanging on the wall above the sink, he was aware that Nancy was staring at him. She said, "You didn't tell me the whole truth, Tom."

He crossed the room to her, fighting the wild hunger that was always in him when he was alone with her. He wanted to take her in his arms, to kiss her and fan into flame the desire which he was sure was in her and needed only a little urging to become a conflagration.

When he was a step from her, he stopped. "Nancy, you know I love you."

"Don't, Tom. Don't say that."

"Wait." He put his hands on her arms, compelled to touch her. He would have kissed her if he had been sure Matthew would stay on the porch, but the old fool might take this exact moment to wheel into the kitchen. "Listen to me, Nancy. It isn't right for you to have to live this way with a man who isn't a man . . ."

She jerked away and backed up, thoroughly angry. "I told you not to say that."

"All right," he said hastily. "But remember this. I want to protect you. You're right that I didn't tell you the whole truth. We're headed for trouble, the worst kind of trouble. So I'm asking you to come and live with me. You and Matthew."

"No, Tom," she said. "We'll stay here."

He heard Matthew's chair coming across

the front room. He walked to the table and sat down. As soon as the meal was finished, he rose abruptly, thanked Nancy, and left. It was dusk now, the air heavy with the rank smell of dust and sage.

He wondered when it would rain, and decided it would not be long. June was seldom as dry and hot as it had been the last week, so the showers which were common through the summer would come soon to break the heat.

Then, slowly, these idle thoughts left his mind and he faced the truth. He should not have forced the issue with Nancy. He was miserable, for now he realized he might have been living with an egotistical dream all these years. Maybe Nancy would never marry him. But he could not bear to face that possibility.

He turned left when he reached the lane that led to Wineglass, the windows of the big house brightly lighted. This was an impulsive decision, one he had not thought out carefully, and he was quite aware that he might be up to his neck in trouble, but at the moment he was reckless and didn't care.

This was a strange feeling for him. He was normally a careful man who planned well, and he realized that his usual caution had been overridden by what Nancy had said. Now he briefly debated with himself, arguing that he was doing the smart thing, that it was time Ben Shortt knew Tom Barren was in the game.

He could think of no better counter-argument, so he dismounted, and stepping up on the porch, pulled the bell cord. He was surprised that there were no guards around the house, but maybe it wasn't surprising. Defense was never a part of Ben Shortt's thinking.

Nikki answered the bell and let him in when he asked to see Shortt. He saw that she was utterly miserable and, as he followed her to Shortt's office, he took the opportunity to say, "Jeff's all right. I was with him this afternoon."

She gave him a quick smile of relief. "I've been worried about him, Mr. Barren. He knows I'm leaving on the stage tomorrow?"

"Yes. Miles Rebus brought word to him."

"I thought he would," she said, and knocking on the door, called, "You have company, Grandpa."

Shortt opened the door, looked at Barren, and scowled. "What the hell do you want?"

"To talk."

Shortt shrugged. "Come in," he said grudgingly.

Barren stepped into the room and closed the door. He studied Shortt a moment, sensing doubt in the other man in spite of his wealth and power, and he knew at once that he was the stronger.

"You're a fool for sending for Sam Marks, Ben," Barren said. "You're a fool for fighting to get poor range you don't need just to satisfy the crazy greed that's eating you."

Shortt sat down. "Crazy or not, I'll stop the rustling that's been going on. Maybe I'll hang you before I'm done."

"Let's be honest," Barren said. "It's your greed that's making you do this. If it was the rustling, you wouldn't have sent for a man like Marks. Now I'm going to say what I came here to say. I'm not in it. Neither is Lacey Dunbar. Most of the rest of them are. If you'd come to me in the first place, I could have given you the information you wanted, but no, you had to be a damned fool and turn Jeff Ardell against you, and then Hank Dolan."

Barren hit a painful nerve end when he said that. Shortt rose and motioned to the door. "Get out of here."

"Your strength is in your money and your crew," Barren said. "Not in you. If you fight me, I'll whip you, but if you work with me, I'll help you and you'll win. Think it

100

over, Ben."

"You help me?" Shortt swore contemptuously. "Get out of here, I told you. I'm guessing you're the bastard that's leading the rustlers."

"You know better," Barren said. "I don't like you and I don't trust you, but you've got something I want. Now do you want to hear my proposition or not?"

"What have I got that you want?"

"Red Mesa. If you win, you'll have all of it. I want Ardell's Rafter A. It's a fair offer in exchange for what I can do for you."

Shortt was red in the face. He shouted, "By God, if you don't get out of here in three seconds, I'll shoot you."

"Shoot," Barren said.

For a moment Shortt hesitated, confused by this unexpected effrontery, then he went for his gun. He stopped its upward movement before it was more than half leveled. Suddenly he found himself looking into the bore of Barren's gun.

"I have every right to kill you, Ben," Barren said. "Old age and rheumatism have got you whipped. Maybe you were a hardcase once, but now you're just a scared old man playing big. That's why you need me. Next time you'll come to me because I'm never coming back to you." He motioned toward

101

the wall. "Lay your gun on the desk and put your back to the wall."

Shortt obeyed, cursing. Barren picked up the gun, opened the door, and backed out of the room as he said, "I'll leave your iron outside. And don't forget something. You owe me your life."

Barren left without trouble, surprised because he thought Shortt would yell for help. But no one else seemed to be around. Barren rode away, deciding that Shortt's men were out hunting for Jeff.

Worry grew in Barren as he rode. Maybe he hadn't done such a smart trick after all. Now Shortt's wrath would certainly fall on him. He hadn't really expected Shortt to take his proposition. It had been an act of bravado to bolster his self-confidence.

He seldom did things that he knew were foolish, but now he saw that this had been worse than foolish. He was worried when he realized why he had done it, why he had even needed some such act to give his self-confidence back to him.

The moon rose and he pushed his horse, wondering if Sam Marks was here yet, if any of Shortt's men were on the mesa. What would they do to him if they caught him?

He sighed with relief when he reached the edge of the mesa and took the road to the bottom of the little valley. He would sleep outside tonight just as a matter of precaution, and again he felt the weakness of doubt. Then he dismissed it.

All he really wanted was to stay alive. That was no weakness, he told himself, and thus, self-assured he turned into the aspens above his buildings and there made his camp.

CHAPTER IX

Jeff rode with Dunbar to the top of the ridge west of Deer Creek until he was sure that the close-growing cedars hid him from Barren's front porch. He pulled up and called, "Wait a minute, Lacey." Hipping around in his saddle, he looked back at the house. Tom Barren sat on his front porch smoking a pipe.

Dunbar asked, "Think he's working for Ben Shortt?"

"Do you know he isn't?" Jeff asked.

"Hell no," Dunbar answered, "but it's a crazy notion."

"Do you trust him?"

"Son, I don't trust nobody but you and God," Dunbar said, "and sometimes I ain't sure about God."

Irritated by Dunbar's answer, Jeff remained silent until Tom Barren rose, mounted his horse, and rode up the east slope to the mesa. "Now where would he be going?" Jeff asked.

"To see Ben Shortt," Dunbar said, laughing.

Jeff held back an angry reply. Dunbar's facetious answer added to his irritation, but that was Lacey Dunbar for you. He seldom took anything seriously. Still, Jeff didn't want to quarrel with him, so he remained silent as they dropped over the ridge and then climbed to Tate Mesa. It was cool here among the spruce trees, and the tension which Jeff had felt for hours began to leave him.

"What do you think of Tom Barren?" Jeff asked. "And don't give me any more of your funny answers."

Jeff's tone was curt, and Dunbar glanced at him, surprised. "You'd better watch out, son," he said. "You'll end up biting yourself, seeing that Ben Shortt ain't handy."

"Hell, you're acting like this was a game," Jeff said. "In case you didn't know it, we're in a fight."

"I know it," Dunbar said. "I'm scared, if that's what you want to hear, but I ain't going around telling folks. When you woke me up in the middle of the night and told me Sam Marks was coming, I got the shakes and I've had 'em ever since."

Dunbar looked straight ahead, his beard

effectively hiding his expression. Jeff, staring at him, had just heard a confession which he had never expected to hear from Lacey Dunbar. Even when they were children, Jeff had never suspected Dunbar of being afraid of anything. But the prospect of Sam Marks hiding in the brush and shooting them down as if they were hunted animals was enough to scare anyone.

"I've got 'em, too," Jeff said. "But what about Tom Barren?"

"I don't know him," Dunbar said. "I don't think anybody does."

Jeff thought about that. His parents probably saw more of Barren than anyone else, but now, considering Dunbar's statement, Jeff felt reasonably certain that neither his father nor mother actually understood Tom Barren. They would have said he was an honest man who was their friend, but that wasn't enough for Jeff. Not at a time like this when you couldn't take chances about who was a friend and who would sell you out when the showdown came.

"I guess not," Jeff said finally. "It's a hell of a note, Lacey. I've lived on Red Mesa almost all my life, and now I can't count on anybody but you and Miles Rebus."

"Every man's stick floats the same way," Dunbar said. "Who can Tom Barren count on?" He cuffed back his hat, laughing again. "Take a look at Ben Shortt. He can count on Steve Lawrence who's afraid to spit without Ben telling him he can, and he can count on his tough hands like Slim Tarrant and Curly Jones as long as he can keep 'em bought. Ain't much satisfaction in either one."

Dunbar shook his head, the laughter leaving him. "It's a tough world, son, a mean, dog-eat-dog, son-of-a-bitching world, and don't you ever doubt it. As far as Tom Barren goes, I wouldn't trust him no farther than I can throw him by his sharp little nose."

"Why?"

"Dunno. Maybe it's 'cause he's so smart. You never know what's going on in his head. Take a man like Floyd Deems. Or Red O'Toole. You know what they're thinking before the thought gets there, but not Tom Barren." Dunbar shrugged. "Why are you interested in him?"

"I keep wondering why he visits the folks," Jeff said. "And why he wants us to sell out and move in with him." He paused, then asked, "You leaving the country tonight?"

"Hell no. We're taking Nikki off the stage tomorrow. Remember?"

"You wanted to pull out . . ."

"Oh, that was last night. I changed my mind today. Fact is, this is the most fun I've had since the wolves ate grandpa."

"How we going to do it?"

"I've been thinking on it," Dunbar said. "We could sashay into town and grab her before she gets on the stage. Trouble is we don't know whether Sam Marks is in town yet or what he'll do if he is. We don't know how many men old Ben will fetch with him when he puts Nikki on the stage. Too many ifs."

"Well, what do we know?"

"Not much. You got any notions?"

"Yeah, I've got one. We'll light out early in the morning and cross Red Mesa, swinging south so nobody will see us. I don't know when the stage hits the Halfway House, but it must be five or six o'clock. Seems to me it's about four hours from the Halfway House to Placerville, and the train gets there before midnight."

"We're gonna tackle the stage at the Halfway House?"

"It's the best thing I can think of. It stops for supper. We'll hide around there somewhere. Soon as we've got her, we'll light out down the river and leave her at my house. The folks'll be glad to have her." Dunbar was silent, and Jeff asked, "Well?"

"I'll think on it," Dunbar said. "If there's any holes in your scheme, we'd best plug 'em."

They went on, riding in silence until they reached Dunbar's cabin and put their horses up. Dunbar cooked supper, and when it was dark, he pulled the heavy shades on his windows and barred the door, then lighted a lamp.

Jeff wasn't sure whether Dunbar was worried about Sam Marks or not. Jeff didn't think the killer represented any immediate danger. He might not have arrived yet. Or if he had, it would take him a day or so to familiarize himself with the country.

Dunbar didn't talk until the dishes were put away. Jeff wanted to tell him to stay out of it, that it wasn't his fight, but he knew there wasn't any use. Dunbar would have been insulted. In spite of his living alone, and his conviction that the world was a tough, dog-eat-dog place, he was a man to whom friendship was a sacred word.

"Let's roll in," Dunbar said. "I figure we'd best pull out of here before sunup. A man walking through the door in daylight makes a prime target."

"You thought about my scheme?" Jeff asked. "See any holes?"

"It's got holes," Dunbar answered, "but I

can't think of anything better, so we'll play it your way."

"What are the holes? Maybe we can plug them like you said."

"No, you can't plug something until you know for sure it's there. We don't know whether old Ben will send some of his tough hands to run herd on her. He might figure she'd make a break for it if she was alone. It ain't likely he'll go, but he might send somebody. That'd mean we've got to take care of whoever is with her."

"I'll take care of her guardian if she's got one," Jeff said. "All I know is that if she gets out of the country, I'll lose her. Shortt will see to that."

"We won't let her out of the country," Dunbar said. "Now there's another angle I don't like. You want to leave her at your house. Maybe you'll have to, but you know Shortt will look there."

"They'll have to hide her. We've got a cave. It's kind of a cellar under the floor. Dad dug it when he built the house because there were still a few bands of Utes that wanted to hunt on the mesa. You never knew when they'd show up or what they'd do. There's a trap door in the floor. By leaving a rug over it, nobody can see it."

"All right," Dunbar said. "I hope to hell

it works."

They left the cabin before the first hint of light showed in the east and slipped into the timber back of the cabin. They crossed the road, swung south, and hit Deer Creek a mile above Tom Barren's ranch. From there they climbed to the mesa.

They circled town, riding slowly and staying in the cedars as much as they could. They saw no one, and as far as they knew, they were not seen. Then, in early afternoon they hit the county road that led from Starbuck to the Halfway House on the San Miguel River.

"Can't hide no more," Dunbar said. "Might as well bull it out."

"Sure," Jeff said. "We'll get dinner at the Halfway House. I hate to fight on an empty stomach."

"Me, too," Dunbar said. "My belly's been howling for an hour."

They followed the narrow road that hung to the south side of the canyon for nearly a mile. Reaching the river, they crossed it and reined up in front of the Halfway House. They tied their horses and went in. Jeff knew the couple that ran the place, but neither was in sight.

A girl came out of the kitchen when they sat down at the long table, frowning in annoyance. "Stage gets here at seven," she said. "That's when we have dinner."

Jeff looked at her, canting his chair back against the wall. She was about sixteen, pretty enough, with yellow-gold hair done up in curls.

"What's your name?" Jeff asked.

"Jenny. I said . . ."

"You sure light the place up," Jeff said. "Last time I was here, Mrs. Hamilton waited on me."

"Milk was sour, wasn't it?" Dunbar said lazily. "They tell me she clabbers the milk just by looking at it."

"Guess she's pretty good at that," Jeff said. "One time I stopped here and Toby Hamilton had a bandage around his head. Claimed his missus whacked him with the frying pan the night before."

"Aw, he's always telling that," Jenny said. "It ain't true."

Jeff tossed a five dollar gold piece on the table. "Is it true you're a good cook, Jenny?"

Her eyes fastened on the gold piece. "That for me?"

He nodded. "See what you can rustle up."

"I'll find something, Mr. . . ."

"James," Jeff said. "Jesse James."

Dunbar tapped his chest. "I'm Frank."

Jenny giggled again. "You're both liars,"

she said, and disappeared into the kitchen.

"So the stage gets here at seven," Dunbar said. "Keep flirting with Jenny. I'm going outside."

He was back in five minutes. "The outhouse is in the brush next to the cliff. We'll hide our horses close to it. We'll holler at Nikki when she comes out, she'll get up behind you, and we'll take off down the river. Nobody'll miss her till the stage leaves."

"If she's alone," Jeff said.

"If she ain't, we'll fix it so she is," Dunbar said.

Jenny brought them cold roast beef, beans, biscuits and coffee. They finished off with dried apple pie and paid her for the meal, Jeff saying, "Let's get to Placerville and hold up the train. We ought to get home with $50,000 about dark, Frank."

"Ought to Jesse," Dunbar agreed, and went out, Jenny giggling behind them.

They mounted and rode downstream, waving to Toby Hamilton who was irrigating a hay field across the river. When they were out of sight, they doubled back, keeping in the brush next to the north wall of the canyon.

They reined up in a thick clump of scrub oak fifty yards from the house, and stepped down. There they waited until they saw the coach coming down the long hill from Red Mesa. It was after seven, the light beginning to fade. A short time later the coach clattered across the bridge, stopped in front of Halfway House, the driver calling, "Supper stop."

The door opened and the first passenger down was Slim Tarrant. He turned and gave Nikki a hand, then went into the house with her. Another man trailed behind them, a hand on gun butt, eyes nervously scanning the brush back of the roadhouse, then he followed Nikki and Tarrant inside.

"He's a new man," Jeff said. "Says his name is Banjo Smith."

"Well now," Dunbar said, "he don't know it, but he's dead meat."

"Or we are," Jeff said. "The way that Smith was looking around, they're expecting something."

Dunbar glanced at him. "Ben Shortt ain't a fool," he said, no laughter in him now. "This is the way I figured he'd play it. Well, we'll see."

CHAPTER X

Sam Marks rode into Starbuck late Tuesday afternoon and turned into Gabby Hart's livery stable. He looked as if he were a drifting cowboy who was hunting a job, dusty and unshaven, a Winchester in the boot, and a walnut-handled .44 in a holster on his right thigh. His age was deceiving, for he had light blue eyes and rosy cheeks that made him look considerably younger than his twenty-seven years.

Marks shook hands with Hart, said in a pleasant voice that he was Bill Brown, and he was looking for a job. "I'm damn near broke," he said. "I need a job and I need it bad."

This was Sam Marks's greatest asset. He bore no resemblance to most people's mental picture of how a calloused killer looked. So, when he appeared in a country where he wasn't known, he was taken for what he appeared to be. Usually he had ample time to do the job he was hired to do, collect his pay, and ride out before folks knew he was the notorious Sam Marks.

Gabby Hart, as anyone in Starbuck would have done, believed what Marks said. "By gosh, Brown, I don't know. I doubt you'll find a riding job till roundup."

"Can't live that long on what I've got," Marks said dismally. "This looks like good cattle country. There oughta be some big outfits hereabouts."

"Just one," Hart told him. "Wineglass. Belongs to an old timer named Ben Shortt. You might ride out there and ask." Hart scratched back of an ear. "If you're broke, you can sleep in the mow. I don't usually allow it on account of most drifters are careless when they smoke, but you don't look to be that kind."

"Thank you for the offer," Marks said gratefully, "but I've got a few dollars. I'll get me a hotel room." He fingered his stubble-covered cheek. "Maybe buy me a shave and a bath. Sooner or later the Lord will provide. That sounds crazy, but He always has."

"It's fine if you believe it," Hart said, "but the Lord's sure been overlooking Red Mesa lately. Even the preacher has to milk a cow and raise chickens and a garden, or he'd starve."

"The cow gives milk," Marks said, "the hens lay eggs, and the garden produces vegetables. I ain't no Bible spouter, you understand. All I know is how it's been with me." He started to leave, then turned back. "Is Ben Shortt likely to show up in town?"

"Not tonight," Hart said. "You'll have to ride out there if you want to see him."

"I ain't et since yesterday," Marks said. "The way I feel, I've done all the riding I'm going to do today. You know of anybody I could get to ride out to Wineglass and carry a note?"

"I've got a kid working for me who'd do it," Hart said, "if you can spare a dollar."

"The way I feel, it'd be worth a dollar," Marks said.

He dug around in his pocket, found a stubby pencil and a tattered piece of paper, and wrote, "I'd like to see you tonight. I'll be in the hotel. Bill Brown." He slipped the note inside an envelope and sealed it. Then he wrote on the outside, "Mr. Short," and handed the envelope to Hart with a silver dollar.

"He spells it with two t's," Hart said. "He's kind of finicky 'bout the way it's spelled."

"Wouldn't do to make him sore to start with," Marks said, and taking the envelope,

117

added a **t** and handed it back to the livery-man. "I'm much obliged."

"Glad to do it," Hart said.

Marks had a bath and shave in Jerry Little's barbershop, took a room at the hotel, and then ate supper. When he returned to his room, it was almost dark, so he lighted a lamp, closed the door, and lay down on the bed, his gun beside him next to his right leg.

He laughed silently, thinking about Ben Shortt who would cuss until he was black in the face when he got the note. The nabobs were all the same, expecting you to come to them and figuring they never had to come to you.

Sam Marks had been carrying on his private feud with the nabobs since he was eighteen and had started using his gun to earn his living. His father, a homesteader in New Mexico, had been shot down in cold blood by a cattle baron's hired killer when Marks was sixteen. His mother had died when he was small, and he had no brothers or sisters. After his father's murder, he began working as a cowhand, having no intention of fighting to save the homestead which had never given his father a decent living anyhow.

Sam Marks learned two things within a

118

few months. First, earning a living by nursing cows was hard work and poorly paid. Second, a great many ranchers, facing ruin from encroaching homesteaders, were not above committing murder to save their range land, but hated to do it themselves.

So Marks started calling himself a range detective. From the time he was eighteen, he had done very well. He never missed a chance to humiliate the men for whom he worked. The more furious he made them, the more he enjoyed it, thus exacting his peculiar revenge upon many cattlemen because of the crime one had committed.

His method of handling Ben Shortt was typical of the way he handled all employers, having thoroughly disliked Shortt when they talked in Denver. Not that he liked anyone. He measured his feelings by various degrees of dislike and he had placed Shortt at the bottom. In the few minutes they had been together, he discovered that Ben Shortt was overburdened by pride, a big, bellowing man who had a way of riding down anyone who got in front of him.

It never occurred to Marks that he was killing men who had been like his father. He hadn't loved his father and he had hated farm work, so he never identified himself with the men he murdered. Besides, he found more often than not that the men he was hired to kill actually were rustlers, and therefore should be rubbed out in the same manner a horse thief was eliminated. The fact that he used a gun instead of a rope was beside the point.

Sam Marks spent nearly an hour enjoying his mental picture of Ben Shortt's towering rage. The man had probably decided to wait until morning, hoping Marks would come to him, but eventually he would beat down his pride. He'd come. They always did.

Marks was right. He heard a man stomp up the stairs and along the hall to his door, then the rap of heavy knuckles. He waited, grinning, until he heard the knock again, then he said, "Come in," his right hand on the bed beside the butt of his gun.

Ben Shortt opened the door, strode in, and slammed the door behind him. He stood staring at Marks, his face white with rage. He said, "Who the hell do you think you are? You could have asked where Wineglass was and ridden out there tonight instead of me coming to town and having to ask at the desk what room you had."

When he was out of breath, he stopped. Marks sat up and laid his gun across his lap. He motioned toward the chair, not saying a word until Shortt sat down. Then he said, "Mr. Shortt, we'll talk when you're polite. Not before. I like politeness in a man."

He said the word "mister" in a mocking tone. Shortt spread his big hands on his knees, the corners of his mouth working. Marks grinned. One man had had a heart attack in a similar situation, and Ben Shortt looked as if he were about to have one now. He labored for breath, then he said, "All right, Marks."

"That's better," Marks said affably. "Now we can talk. I'm not a man to beat around the bush. I'm a killer. You want men killed. Who are they and where will I find them?"

The words rekindled the rage in Shortt and he jumped up, started to say something, and then sat down again. Marks tapped the wall. "Thin, Mr. Shortt. Keep your voice down."

At least thirty seconds passed before Shortt could control his voice enough to say, "I want a range detective. That's what I thought I hired. It's up to you to gather evidence and turn it over to me. Then the law will take its course."

"You can lie to yourself, Mr. Shortt," Marks said, "but don't do it to me. You wanted a stranger to knock over the men you figure have been getting your cattle, then you pay off, and he leaves the country. All right, I'm your huckleberry."

"By God, you're . . ."

Marks raised a hand. "I shouldn't say it so plainly, should I? Well, we're grown men, Mr. Shortt. Let's act that way. And another thing. The fact that you asked the hotel clerk which room I had is enough, I think, to keep you from double-crossing me, if something goes wrong. If I hang, you will hang beside me."

Shortt sat there, staring at Marks and hating him, but fearing him, too. Then Marks said, "Who are the men?"

"We'll talk about it tomorrow," Shortt answered. "There are two other ranchers on the mesa who are with me in this. They should be here when we discuss your job."

"We'll talk about it now," Marks said pleasantly. "You were the man who hired me and you're the man who will pay me." He rolled a smoke, his revolver still in his lap. "As I remember it, you had three neighbors who were backing your scheme."

"One of them quit Sunday," Shortt said. "I explained what we were going to do, but he wouldn't stand for it. We tried to nail him, but he threw a few shots at the house and got clear."

"He knows I'm . . ." Marks stopped, unable to believe this. "You mean he's running around telling everyone you sent for me?"

"Not everyone," Shortt said. "He ain't had time. Don't worry. We'll get him."

Marks lighted his cigarette. "You are a fool, Mr. Shortt. What you have just told me makes it necessary to double my rate. I'll have to work fast and light a shuck out of the country. Usually I take half of my pay before the job, the rest after I'm finished. In this case, you will pay all of my fee before I start. One thousand dollars a man. Do you have the money?"

Shortt was beaten. He didn't even argue. He said, "At home. I'll bring it to you in the morning."

"That's better. Do you have the map of the country I told you to get?"

Shortt nodded and drew a folded sheet of paper from his pocket. He sat there, tapping it against his leg. "I don't like the way you talk about this, Marks. I'm not a cold-blooded killer. I want evidence that these men are rustlers."

"You are a cold-blooded killer," Marks said. "So am I. Why be mealy-mouthed about it? But if you want evidence, I can get it. Men like this always eat their big neighbor's beef. I'd say the odds are ten to one I can find a Wineglass hide."

123

"All right, find a hide before you take any steps." Shortt unfolded the map and laid it on the bed. He pointed out the major landmarks, then his finger stopped at Tom Barren's place. "This man, his name is Barren, is the smartest of the bunch. I think he's their leader." His finger moved west to Lacey Dunbar's cabin. "This fellow's name is Dunbar. Outside of raising a few horses and working during roundup, he does nothing for a living. He's in it up to his thieving neck."

"With them two dead, the rest will get out of the country. Is that it?"

"I think so," Shortt said reluctantly.

Marks nodded. "See that I get the money in the morning."

Shortt hesitated, then he pointed to the Rafter A. "A bastard named Jeff Ardell lives here. He's the one who ran out on me Sunday afternoon. He wants to marry my granddaughter, but I'll kill him myself before I'll let that happen. Get him, too. The trouble is he's not at home. You may have trouble finding him."

"If your boys who know the country couldn't find him, how do you expect me to?"

"It may take time," Shortt admitted.

"Bring $2,000," Marks said. "If I'm lucky

and nail your man Ardell, I'll collect for that later. After the way you've balled things up, I won't have time to hang around and hunt for anybody."

"All right," Shortt said heavily.

Marks rose. "Good-night, Mr. Shortt. I wish there were more men like you who can afford their murders."

He stood there, smiling, his blue eyes blandly innocent. Shortt wheeled and went out, slamming the door shut. Marks laughed aloud, and turned the key in the lock.

This was the first time in Marks's career when his potential victims had been warned. He would have to work fast. Tomorrow he would locate where Barren and Dunbar lived, maybe get one of them and finish the next day, then light out for the Utah border.

Part of his success was due to the mystery which surrounded him. No one knew him well. Few recognized him by sight. More than that, he never left evidence behind him. At least none that had been found. And no one had ever witnessed any of his killings.

Some said it was the luck of the devil, but Marks laid it to careful planning. Now, after nine years as an exterminator, stories about him had grown until he had become a legend. That was why men like Ben Shortt continued to hunt him up.

He took off his clothes and went to bed. His revolver, as usual, was on the bed beside him. Being a light sleeper, he woke at the slightest noise, a faculty which had saved his life on more than one occasion. He had never been one to worry, but now he was uneasy. The men he was to kill would be watching for him, they would know he was in the country.

He'd be smart to take Shortt's money and ride out after the fool had bungled everything the way he had. But he wouldn't. He had never cheated a man with whom he had made a deal. He wouldn't start with Ben Shortt.

CHAPTER XI

Jeff and Lacey Dunbar, watching from their hiding place in the scrub oak behind the Halfway House, saw that Nikki, Slim Tarrant and Banjo Smith were the only passengers on the stage. Toby Hamilton came in from the hay meadow on the other side of the river and took care of the horses.

"What'n hell are they doing?" Dunbar whispered. "I didn't think they'd fool around this long."

Jeff's hand closed over Dunbar's arm. "There she is." Then he groaned. Nikki came around the Halfway House and disappeared behind it. Banjo Smith followed her to the corner and stopped, his gaze nervously sweeping the rim above the canyon, then the road, and finally the brush along the river.

"Get the horses," Jeff said. "I'll take care of Smith. Pull Nikki up behind you and bust the breeze getting out of here."

"The hell," Dunbar said. "I'll take care of Smith . . ."

"Do what I tell you," Jeff said sharply, and plowing through the brush into the open, called, "Hook the moon, Smith."

The Wineglass man jumped and wheeled. He recognized Jeff and went for his gun. He expected trouble and was keyed up for it, yet when it came, he was not prepared. Or he was keyed up too much. His gun caught in his holster, and Jeff yelled, "Drop it, Smith, or I'll kill you."

Toby Hamilton dived inside the barn. Jeff heard Dunbar behind him with the horses, heard Nikki cry out, then Smith had his gun free. Jeff yelled again, "Drop it." But Smith had either lost his head or underestimated Jeff. His gun kept coming up. Jeff fired, the bullet knocking Smith back on his heels. The Wineglass man pulled the trigger, a wild shot that kicked up dust between them, but he didn't go down.

Jeff ran toward him. Smith bent forward, one hand holding to his side, the other gripping the gun as he strained to bring it level. Jeff's second bullet caught him in the neck, slashing his jugular vein. He fell, blood pumping out of his throat in a great stream.

Whirling, Jeff ran to his horse and swung into the saddle just as Slim Tarrant charged around the corner of the house. Jeff threw a shot at him that splintered a board level with his head. Reversing himself, Tarrant dived frantically for cover. Jeff holstered his gun and dug in his spurs. He raced downriver, skirting the brush until he reached the road.

Behind Jeff, Tarrant bellowed, "Hamilton, get me a horse."

Jeff caught up with Nikki and Dunbar a moment later, Nikki riding behind Dunbar, her skirt pulled high, her arms around his waist. They went this way for a mile, Jeff knowing they couldn't hold so fast a pace, and knowing, too, that Tarrant would be after them.

A quarter of a mile farther downstream the river made a sharp turn, the road swinging briefly away from the bank and running between two sandstone pillars. Jeff yelled, "Pull up, Lacey."

Jeff reined in behind the pillar on the south side of the road and stopped out of sight of anyone coming from the east. Dunbar wheeled his horse, staring at Jeff as if he were out of his head, then rode back slowly.

"You gone clean loco, son?" Dunbar demanded. "Tarrant will be on our tail in five minutes."

"I'm counting on that," Jeff said. "Get off

the road."

As soon as Dunbar pulled up beside Jeff's mount, Jeff lifted his hands to Nikki. She fell into them, suddenly limp. Everything had happened so fast that she had been too shocked to fully understand what it was all about, but now her arms came around him and she began to cry.

"Hang on," he said, and kissed her. He pushed her against the sandstone. "Don't move. We'll handle Tarrant when he gets here."

"My God, Jeff, have you gone out of your mind?" Dunbar asked.

"All right, all right," Jeff said. "We'll argue about it tomorrow. I don't want Tarrant killed if I can help it, but I'm not going to have him on our tail all night. You get over on the other side of the road. Keep your gun in your hand. When he's almost here, jump out and tell him to get his hands up. I'll yank him out of his saddle, then you grab the reins."

"Why don't you want to kill him?" Dunbar demanded.

"I've killed one man tonight. Isn't that enough?"

Dunbar stood there, scowling. The light was thin, shadow steadily deepening here in the bottom of the canyon. It would soon be dark, at least until the moon came up. If they were lucky, they could reach the trail that led up the south wall of the canyon to the Rafter A while it was still light.

When Dunbar didn't move, Jeff said irritably, "Go on."

"You don't want to kill him, you say," Dunbar said. "Well, I'll tell you something. It's not enough. Not near enough. What do you think Tarrant's going to do when he sees me?"

"Nothing. He won't be riding with a gun in his hand."

"Shoot him out of his saddle and be done with it," Dunbar said sullenly. "It's what Tarrant would do to you."

"Maybe, but we're not him. Besides, I aim to send him back to Wineglass with a message. Now will you do what I tell you?"

Dunbar obeyed reluctantly. Jeff crouched against the side of the sandstone across the road from Dunbar, listening. A minute or two later he heard the approaching hammer of hoofs. Tarrant was coming fast. Rocks started rolling behind Jeff. He turned to see Nikki working her way up the side of the cliff. A moment later she crawled out on top of the pillar and lay flat.

Jeff started to tell her to come down, then realized she was safer up there than she would be beside him if there was any shooting. He asked, "See anything?"

"Yes. He's alone."

"Good."

He had time to get up there beside her. From that position he could shoot Tarrant without running the slightest risk of Tarrant shooting back. As Dunbar had said, it was exactly what Tarrant would have done. Still, knowing this, Jeff could not bring himself to dry gulch Slim Tarrant.

The Wineglass foreman was close now. Close enough. Jeff motioned for Dunbar to make his move, but for a terrifying second he thought Dunbar had lost his nerve. He hadn't. His sense of timing was better than Jeff's. When Dunbar lunged into the road, Tarrant was barely on the upstream side of the gap.

"Pull up," Dunbar yelled. "Get your meat hooks up."

Tarrant's horse skidded to a stop, dust boiling up around him. Cursing, he drew his gun as he rolled off his horse on Jeff's side. He must have forgotten about Jeff, or supposed he had gone on with Nikki, leaving Dunbar behind to see they weren't followed.

Jeff was on Tarrant before he hit the ground. Dunbar had the reins and was hanging on in spite of the animal's lunging. A hoof grazed Jeff's head, then Dunbar pulled the horse off the road. Jeff kept astraddle of the squirming, swearing Tarrant.

Dunbar yelled, "Ride 'em, cowboy."

Jeff twisted the gun out of Tarrant's hand and threw it into the brush. He got to his feet, saying, "Take it easy and you won't get hurt. I want you to take a message to Ben."

But Tarrant was in no mood to take it easy. Coming up off the road, he rushed Jeff, his fists swinging. Jeff met him headlong, taking a windmill right to his chest and hammering Tarrant in return on the side of the head, a looping blow that had the power of a mule kick.

Tarrant went down, scooting in the dust and gravel. Jeff dropped on his back, knees driving breath out of the bigger man, but it didn't stop him. He rolled over, dislodging Jeff, and grabbing up a rock twice as big as his fist, threw it at Jeff.

The rock struck Jeff on the shoulder, spinning him partly around. Dunbar yelled, "Stay clear, Jeff. I'll shoot the bastard."

"No," Jeff shouted, and closed with Tarrant, driving a heel down against the man's instep.

Tarrant let out a bawl of pain and

slammed an elbow against Jeff's throat, the blow momentarily stopping his breathing. Tarrant got both arms around him, trying to squeeze hard enough to smother his blows. They wrestled that way for a time, Tarrant doing his best to ram Jeff against the sandstone pillar.

Dunbar, his gun raised to bring it down across Tarrant's head, followed a step behind, but now Jeff had a handful of Tarrant's hair, and Dunbar would have broken Jeff's hand if he'd swung the gun barrel.

Jeff yanked, tilting Tarrant's head so that his chin was exposed. Jeff got his right hand free. He swung his fist to Tarrant's jaw, and swung again. Tarrant went limp. The pressure slackened around Jeff's middle. He released his grip on the man's hair and stepped away. Tarrant, his knees rubbery, went down and lay still.

Nikki slid to the ground in a shower of rocks. She ran to Jeff, crying, "You all right, Jeff? You all right?"

He leaned against the sandstone, still laboring for breath. He said, "Sure," and wiped a sleeve across his face. Dunbar holstered his gun, savagely angry. "Why didn't you let me kill him? Now he'll have another chance at us." He dug a toe into Tarrant's ribs. "Get up. You ain't hurt much."

"Let him alone, Lacey," Jeff said.

"Well, by God, I'll tell you again," Dunbar shouted. "One man ain't enough." He threw up his hands in disgust. "We'll have blood all over Red Mesa until it's a hell of a lot redder'n it is now, and you want to keep this booger alive. Why? Tell me why."

Tarrant was on his knees, his eyes glassy. Jeff, looking down, knew that Dunbar was right. Still, Jeff was the one who had killed Banjo Smith, the first man he had ever killed in his life. It would be a long time before he forgot the sight of blood pumping from the man's bullet-torn throat.

"If you don't know, I can't tell you why, Lacey," Jeff said. "Let's pull off his boots."

Dunbar gave Tarrant a vicious backhanded blow on the face that knocked him flat. Dunbar took one boot and Jeff the other, and yanked until they came off. Dunbar threw the one he had into the river; Jeff tossed the other one into the brush.

"You're walking back in your socks," Jeff said. "We'll turn the horse loose after a while. Tell Toby that."

Tarrant's eyes were still glassy, but he was conscious enough to hear what Jeff said. "Shoot him," Dunbar said. "One of these days you'll be damned sorry you didn't."

Jeff glanced at Dunbar's face and brought

his gaze back to Tarrant. He had never seen his friend look this way before. At that moment Lacey Dunbar was a wolf with the smell of blood in his nostrils. He would have placed the muzzle of his gun to Tarrant's head and blown the man's brains out if Jeff had let him.

"Go back to Wineglass," Jeff told Tarrant. "Tell Ben to pull his hounds off my tail and get Sam Marks out of the country. And tell him Nikki will be all right." He took the man by the shoulder and pulled him to his feet. "Start walking."

Tarrant was too badly beaten to have any energy to curse the man who had whipped him. He started down the road, lurching like a drunk.

"We'd better ride," Jeff said.

They mounted without another word, Dunbar still furious, and presently reached the switchback trail that led to the mesa. Jeff had been leading the horse Tarrant had borrowed from Hamilton. He gave the animal a cut with the bridle, knowing the animal would go back to the Halfway House.

They started up the trail, daylight nearly gone. Jeff felt Nikki's arms around him, felt her tremble, and he wondered if she would ever get over the terror of the last hour.

Then his hatred for Ben Shortt grew until it was a fever in him. Killing Slim Tarrant wasn't the answer. Killing Ben Shortt was. His tough crew couldn't save him. And neither could Sam Marks.

CHAPTER XII

The moon was up before they reached the mesa. Lacey Dunbar had not said a word all the way to the top. This was the break up, Jeff thought. Dunbar would leave the country which was what he had wanted to do all the time, and Jeff would be left with allies like Tom Barren and Red O'Toole, men he could not count on.

Jeff understood Dunbar's resentment and therefore did not blame him. By nature Dunbar was a primitive and savage man, as much wolf as human. His manner of life had taught him long ago that if he was attacked, he must fight back with the same brutality with which his assailant had made the attack.

Jeff had not been raised that way. Now, with his own fury cooled, he was able to look at the situation objectively, and so reached a conclusion he had never been able to honestly face before. The truth was he had too much of his father in him to kill a man unless he was forced to, even if that man was Slim Tarrant.

Reaching the top of the mesa, Jeff said, "We'll separate, Lacey. I'm taking Nikki to the Rafter A."

Silence for a time, and Jeff thought Dunbar was going to ride off and say nothing, but presently he said, "Good idea. They'll do some tracking in the morning. If we give 'em two trails, they may take a while to figure out which one Nikki was on."

"Chances are they will," Jeff agreed.

But he knew that time meant little. Ben Shortt would certainly guess that Nikki would be with the Ardells. The only other place she could go would be to town where Miles Rebus would keep her. Shortt would look there, too.

"I'll wait for you at Barren's place," Dunbar said, and swung to the west.

Dunbar wasn't quitting, Jeff thought, and was relieved. He rode toward the Rafter A for a few minutes, then turned east to cross a stretch of hard pan which would delay Tarrant if he did the tracking. On the other hand, Tarrant or whoever it was might light out straight for the house and not follow trail.

Even if the trackers followed Dunbar's

trail as far as Barren's place and lost most of one day, it wouldn't make any difference in the long run. Sooner or later the Wineglass men would come to the Rafter A. What happened after that depended on how well Jeff's folks could resist pressure. Was it possible for a woman and an invalid to hold out against Slim Tarrant?

Jeff wasn't sure. He reined up. "I've been wrong, Nikki. They're bound to look for you here. I can't keep you with me because I'll be running and dodging all over the country. Maybe we'd better turn around and try to get over the divide to Montrose."

"No," she said. "We'd run onto some Wineglass men on the plateau."

She was probably right. Shortt wouldn't bring in all the men from the cow camp. Worse yet was the fact that Jeff would be leaving Dunbar and Miles Rebus and his folks to face Ben Shortt, while he was off running like a rabbit.

So he rode on, the lights of the Rafter A ranch house ahead of him. "You're right," he said. "Nothing else we can do."

"I'd like to stay with your folks, Jeff," she said. "You know, I've never seen your father. I want to know him. He must be a great man."

"He was once," Jeff said, then added

140

quickly, "he still is, as far as that goes. It's just that he can't get around."

"I know," she said. "Grandpa never talks about him, but I always suspected he was afraid of your father."

It would work out all right, Jeff thought. It had to. There was no choice. He thought of going on to Tom Barren's place and leaving Nikki there, but he gave up the notion. Barren lived alone. No, the Rafter A was the only place he could take her.

He reined up behind the barn and dismounted. He remained there a few minutes, listening, Nikki beside him. He didn't think Shortt would have anyone here now, for Shortt would not consider the possibility that Tarrant and Banjo Smith would fail to put Nikki on the train at Placerville.

Still, Jeff would be foolish to step into a trap if there was one. So, impelled by a caution which was new to him, he eased around the barn, leading Nikki by a hand, and stopped again when he rounded the corner.

He heard Nikki's breathing, then was aware that his own was just as loud, and again a wild fury possessed him. Here he was, being hunted like an animal and doing something which could bring disaster to his parents, yet having no choice.

"Come on," he said roughly.

They started across the yard, the moon high enough in the sky so that the house and outbuildings stood out almost as clearly as they would have in full daylight. The windows weren't covered. Long before they reached the front door, he could see his mother knitting beside the walnut stand that held two kerosene lamps.

It was a plain invitation for murder, Jeff told himself angrily. A man who was capable of sending for Sam Marks was capable of anything, even ordering the murder of Nancy Ardell, and certainly of Matthew Ardell who had probably been sitting in his wheel chair beside the lamp earlier in the evening.

Jeff had not seen or heard anything to warn him, but now the warning was there, a weird stirring along his spine, a pressure against his chest, a clammy film of sweat on his forehead. As far as he knew, nothing tangible had happened. Perhaps his fears had finally got the best of him.

He said, "Run," and spun away from Nikki, knowing that regardless of what had caused this haunting sense of danger, he could not ignore it. He was a good five feet from Nikki when a gun was fired from the shadows behind the house, a long tongue of gun-flame flashing into the moonlight, the roar of the shot terrifyingly loud after the silence.

Jeff dropped flat on the ground. The slug had come close. Too close. Nikki had obeyed without question and was in the house. Jeff yelled, "Blow out the lamps." Now, lying on his belly he had his gun in his hand, but he had no idea what sort of protection the ambusher had. Jeff would be wasting lead if he fired, and would succeed only in pinpointing his position.

The man opened up again, slugs kicking up the dust all around Jeff. It was too far to go back to the barn. There was no protection out here in the yard, so he couldn't stay here. That left only one thing to do. He lunged toward the corner of the house, shouting, "I'm coming in, Ma." But he didn't go in. He raced around the house as the lamp winked out, cleared the corner and sprinted along the east wall, his gun still in his hand.

He had no time to plan, but he had a notion that if the bushwhacker thought he was inside, he would show himself. He might try to break into the house. Or give it up and run.

When Jeff reached the back of the house, he saw he had been right. A man was sprinting from where he had been hiding toward the woodshed. Jeff fired. The man stumbled and fell. He threw a wild shot at Jeff. He got up and tried to run, but he was slow. Jeff thought he must have caught the bush-whacker in the leg.

Jeff didn't know how many shots the man had fired, but his gun must be empty or nearly so. Unless he was carrying a second gun, Jeff had him.

"Hold up," Jeff called.

But the man had no intention of holding up. He fired three shots, the last one close. He hadn't had time to reload, so he must be carrying two guns. Jeff ran toward him, knowing it was kill or be killed.

The backyard between Jeff and the dry gulcher was filled with alternate patches of moonlight and shadow, giving an unreal and distorted appearance to anything that moved. That, coupled with the agony the man was suffering from his wound, must have been the reason he had missed those last shots.

Jeff held his fire until he was close, then he stopped and fired twice. He nailed the man with at least one bullet, for the fellow who had not given up trying to reach the shed gave out a high yell and fell forward past the corner of the building.

Jeff ran toward him, holding back the last

two shells. But he didn't need them. The man was dead, a gun still in his hand. Jeff lighted a match, and cupping one hand around the flame, held it close to the man's face. Buffalo Runyan, another tough hand Shortt had taken on last summer when he'd hired Curly Jones.

Jeff holstered his gun, and pulling Runyan's gun out of his slack fingers, slipped it under his own waistband. He leaned against the wall of the shed, breathing hard. Banjo Smith at the Halfway House, now Buffalo Runyan.

Funny, Jeff thought, laughing funny if there was any laughter left in a man. He and Dunbar and Barren and the rest were worried about Sam Marks, but so far no one had seen Marks. The men Jeff had killed were cowhands Shortt had hired less than a year ago.

Thinking about it, Jeff remembered that Slim Tarrant had rodded Wineglass for only two years. Shortt had fired his old foreman at that time, giving no reason for it. Since then he had let other men go, making room for the Banjo Smiths and the Buffalo Runyans.

He found Runyan's horse behind the shed. He lifted the body into the saddle and lashed it down, realizing that Ben Shortt had planned his moves for some time, at least for the three years that Matthew Ardell had been an invalid.

Suddenly Jeff thought of Nikki and his folks who were in the house and could not have known what had happened. He called, "Nikki! Ma! I'm all right. Light the lamps."

He led Runyan's horse to where he had left his mount behind the barn. His first thought had been to turn Runyan's animal loose so he would take the body back to Wineglass. Now he changed his mind. He'd let Shortt worry about what had happened to Buffalo Runyan. Stepping up, he rode north toward the rim of the San Miguel Canyon, leading Runyan's horse.

When he reached the canyon, he untied the body and heaved it over the rim. He threw the saddle into the canyon, removed the bridle and gave the horse a clout on the rump. Mounting, he rode back to the Rafter A, finding grim satisfaction in the mental picture of Ben Shortt's face when Runyan's horse showed up at Wineglass, perhaps close to the time when Slim Tarrant rode in.

Chapter XIII

Nikki ran to Jeff the instant he came into the house. He held her hard in his arms, nodding at his mother who stood in the middle of the room beside the walnut stand. "It's all right," he said. "The man's dead."

Nikki looked up. "Who is it?"

"Buffalo Runyan."

"I won't cry over him," Nikki said.

"Nikki said you haven't eaten since early in the afternoon," Nancy Ardell said. "I'll fix you something."

Matthew wasn't in sight. Jeff asked. "Dad go to bed?"

His mother nodded. "He gets tired awfully quick anymore."

Jeff laid his hat on the stand and put the gun beside it that he had taken from Runyan. Runyan had probably dropped his first gun somewhere between the woodpile and the shed. Then he remembered that the man had fired three shots with this gun. It was a

.45, the same caliber gun that Jeff carried. He ejected the empties and taking three shells from his belt, thumbed them into the cylinder. He put the gun down again, glancing at Nikki who still stood beside him.

"This .45 is pretty heavy for a woman," Jeff said, "but you can use it if you have to."

"I can and I will," she said. "Where is this going to end?"

"I wish I knew." He kissed her and patted her shoulder. "Go help Ma. I want to talk to Dad."

She nodded and went into the kitchen. Jeff turned to the door of Matthew's bedroom, dreading this interview and yet knowing he could not avoid it. Matthew lay in bed, his hands folded on top of the quilt.

"It was a relief when you hollered," Matthew said.

"I got him and he didn't get me," Jeff said. "It was that simple."

"Sit down," Matthew said. "I want to hear about Sunday afternoon."

Jeff drew his chair up to the bed and told Matthew what had happened. As he talked, he realized he had never seen his father as frail as he was now. When he finished, he asked, "Did Nikki tell you about Banjo Smith and Slim Tarrant?"

Matthew nodded. "What are you going to

do now?"

"I'm not sure. Lacey's waiting for me at Tom Barren's place. We'll decide after I get there." He got up and walking to the bureau, opened the top drawer and took out his father's Peacemaker, a gun Matthew had owned as long as Jeff could remember, even before they had come to the mesa. He saw that it was loaded, and returning to the bed, laid it beside Matthew. "Keep this with you. Next time I might not be around."

Matthew picked the gun up, hefted it, and laid it back on the bed. "It's no good, Jeff," he said. "You've heard me say more than once that anything a man can accomplish by violence he can accomplish better by other means."

"How could I have got Nikki away from the Halfway House without violence?" Jeff asked. "And how else should I have handled Buffalo Runyan just now?"

Matthew closed his eyes, his clawlike hands clasped into bony fists. He said, "You're right. Ever since I was twenty years old I've tried to believe what I just said. I've been able to until tonight."

He opened his eyes and looked at Jeff. "I'll tell you something even your mother doesn't know. You're not like me, Jeff, so maybe these killings won't do to you what a couple of killings did to me when I was twenty years old. That was before I met your mother.

"I killed two men in Trinidad. It was a pretty rough town in those days. They would have killed me if I hadn't killed them. But knowing that didn't help. I was close to being crazy for a while. That's why I decided that I would never use a gun again."

Looking down at Matthew's face, filled with agony as the old and terrible memories returned to him, Jeff realized how much like his father he was. He said, "We're more alike than either one of us knew. Otherwise I would have killed Slim Tarrant like Lacey wanted to. I'm not sure yet I was right."

"You were right," Matthew said. "As you get older and have time to look back, you'll realize how right you were. That's why I've lived the way I have, and why I've done things you didn't understand. Sometimes it seems to me that the Lord never intended for fathers and sons to understand each other. I guess I wanted you to be like me, but what I failed to take into account was the fact that circumstances make it impossible for us to be alike."

Jeff nodded, for this was something he had thought about, too. He said, "If you had been able to get around, you would have stopped Ben. What should I have done that I didn't?"

"Nothing," Matthew said. "Remember I was the first man on the mesa. I went out of my way to help the newcomers out. Maybe they all owed me a debt of one kind or another. But Ben was different. I suppose he hated me all this time because he was beholden to me on account of that first winter."

"Nikki says he was afraid of you."

"I think he was, crazy as that sounds," Matthew said. "Maybe it was because I could get men to follow me. Ben knew I could turn everyone in the county against him, and I would if he had turned his wolf loose then. Public opinion was something Ben Shortt couldn't fight."

Jeff nodded, thinking his father was right. Matthew had a capacity for leadership, but when Jeff thought about the meeting at Red O'Toole's place, he knew he lacked that capacity. Maybe it would come with age. Now there was nothing to do but fight, and that, Jeff knew, was one thing he could do.

"I can't tell you how much Nikki means to me," Jeff said. "Or what it would do to me if you and Ma were killed. You'll have trouble, but it'll be worse if I stay, so it's up to you to look after Nikki and Ma."

"Nikki's a fine girl," Matthew said. "We're proud to have her for a daughter. I'll take care of her."

From the doorway Nikki called, "Your supper's ready, Jeff."

"Thanks. I'll look in before I leave, Dad."

Jeff joined Nikki, and walked with her to the kitchen, an arm around her. "You heard Dad say you were a fine girl?"

She looked up at him, smiling. "I heard, and to me that's a fine compliment. Oh Jeff, you don't know how wonderful it is to be here. Just in these few minutes I've found something I never had when I lived with my parents, or when I was in school in Denver. Not after I came to Wineglass, either."

"What is it? Maybe it's something I never found."

"Of course you have," she answered. "It's not anything you can put a name to. Love, I suppose. Faith. Trust. Oh, I don't know. Maybe it's a willingness to give to someone else. That's something Grandpa could never do."

Jeff sat down and began to eat, his mother standing near the stove. Nikki dropped into a chair across the table from Jeff, a cup of coffee in front of her.

When Jeff finished, he rose. "I've got to ride. I don't know what will happen, or

152

when I can get back. Ma, keep your windows covered at night. If anyone rides in, put Nikki in the cave."

"Now quit worrying," Nancy said. "Even Ben Shortt wouldn't harm a couple of women and Matthew crippled up like he is."

"Slim Tarrant would," Jeff said.

He stepped into the bedroom and told Matthew good-by. He kissed Nikki, gave his mother a quick hug, and left. He hated good-bys; he had said all he could to warn his parents. Now, he had to give all of his attention to staying alive. He had hurt Ben Shortt, hurt him so badly that Shortt would redouble his efforts to find him.

Jeff headed west across the mesa, riding fast, prodded by the fear that Shortt might have men hunting for him now. Riding in the moonlight was almost as dangerous as being out in the daytime. Now and then he stopped to listen, but it was not until he reached the western side of Red Mesa that he heard riders to the north.

For a time he fought the urge to make a run for Barren's place but he knew the sound of his horse would bring pursuit if these were Wineglass men. He had no idea how large a party it was. Possibly a dozen. If so, he would bring disaster to Dunbar and Barren as well as himself. Unwilling to take that chance, he reined off into a brush-choked arroyo, dismounted, and stood by his horse's head.

The men passed not far to the north. From the sound of their passage, he judged the party was a big one, eight or ten men. Too many to fight, so he knew he had done the right thing.

Jeff waited until he could no longer hear them, then he crawled through the brush to the lip of the bank. He couldn't see them. Deciding it was safe to go on, he returned to his horse, mounted, and rode on toward Barren's ranch.

When he dropped down off the mesa, he saw there were lights in Barren's house, the windows uncovered, and he cursed Barren's carelessness.

He splashed across the creek, calling, "Tom. Lacey."

The door opened and Barren stepped out, followed by Dunbar who bellowed, "I'm real joyful to see you, son."

"I'm joyful to see both of you idiots alive," Jeff said. "Tom, keep a lamp going and your windows uncovered and you'll get shot through the head."

Barren stood there, sullenly silent. Dunbar strode out of the house and mounted.

154

They rode on toward Tate Mesa, Dunbar laughing softly. He said, "Jeff you insulted Tom. He sure didn't like it. I'll bet that's the first time in his life he was ever called an idiot."

CHAPTER XIV

Tom Barren's boiling point had always been low, and age and increasing dignity had brought it even lower. He stood on his front porch in the light, refusing to give Jeff the satisfaction of seeing him retreat and thus admit he was an idiot just as Jeff had charged. *He was.* That was what got under his hide.

Last night Barren had been careful to sleep in the aspens. When he woke, he had scouted the brush to determine if anyone was hiding. But tonight he'd stood out there in the light with Lacey Dunbar, making a target as big as a house. He'd thought about it, but he hadn't wanted to appear afraid in front of Dunbar.

Funny how he felt strong when he was with some men. When he'd faced Ben Shortt in his office yesterday, for instance. But Lacey Dunbar wasn't afraid of anything, and when Barren was with him, he always felt futile and inadequate.

When Barren was sure the two men were out of sight, he stepped back into the house and blew out the lamp. Picking up his blankets, he slipped out through the back door. Maybe these precautions were foolish. There simply was no defense against a dry gulcher who would hide in the brush and shoot a man in the back.

He slept very little that night. Being called an idiot still rankled. Well, Jeff Ardell wasn't going to live long enough to call many people idiots. Dunbar had told Barren about taking Nikki from the Halfway House. That made Jeff a dead man.

Sooner or later Barren's thinking returned to Sam Marks. Barren's visit with Shortt on Wineglass had been an act of sheer bravado. The more Barren thought about it, the more he saw that his position was untenable.

Barren should have killed Shortt when he had a chance. He couldn't count on getting another one, so he considered Sam Marks and wondered how the man could be used. He was undoubtedly a heartless killer, but he was also a mercenary bastard.

Barren had nearly $2,000 in the bank. He could borrow more if he had to. The question was whether Marks was in town. Once he was on the prowl, he would be hard to find, but if Barren could catch him in town, he'd find a way to talk to him.

Barren got up at dawn, tired and cranky. He scouted the brush, and finding nothing suspicious, went into the house and cooked breakfast. A wind was blowing down the creek. The house creaked under the gusts and Barren jumped with every sound.

He couldn't eat his breakfast. He got a cup of coffee down, then went to the corral, his eyes studying the aspens while chills like tiny electric shocks went up and down his spine. He saddled up, slipped his Winchester into the boot and mounted. He was relieved when he crossed the creek and climbed to the mesa without anything happening.

When he reached town, he tied up on the south side of the street, making a careful survey of the short business block. The hour was still early, the bank closed, the stores just being opened. His horse was the only one tied at any of the hitch rails.

His stomach was queazy. It wouldn't take much to bring his cup of coffee up. He swallowed, wondering how he would go about finding Marks and what he would say if he did find him. The first thing, he decided, was to have a look at the hotel register.

He hadn't been on the north side of the street for a long time, but to hell with that.

He strode across the street, moving fast, and went into the hotel. Glancing into the dining room, he saw that a dozen or more people were having breakfast. The clerk wasn't at the desk, so Barren spun the register and ran his finger down the list of names.

Three people had registered Monday, one woman and two drummers Barren knew. Just one man on Tuesday. Bill Brown. Barren turned away, disappointed. Then it struck him. Sam Marks would not use his own name. Bill Brown and Sam Marks were very likely one and the same.

Barren took a chair in a corner of the lobby, picked up a week-old Denver newspaper and held it in front of his face. Five minutes passed, maybe ten, then the clerk came into the lobby from the dining room beside a young fellow, smooth-shaven with the apple-red cheeks of a healthy youngster.

"I dunno, Mr. Brown," the clerk said. "If Ben Shortt's filled up, you might just as well be riding."

"I reckon I had," the other said. "I'm the best damned bronc twister in the country, but getting started some place where they don't know you ain't easy."

"No, it ain't," the clerk agreed. "Come fall . . ."

"Hell, I can't live on air that long. That son of a bitch of a Ben Shortt makes me so mad that every time I spit, the ground smokes. I had a letter of introduction from an outfit below Montrose. Shortt knows 'em, but he didn't take no stock in the letter."

Brown started up the stairs, then stopped when the clerk said, "Ben was in to see you last night. Came in again early this morning. I didn't figure he'd make a couple of rides to town unless he had use for you."

Brown laughed. "I sent for him. Told him I had an important letter for him. I didn't see him last night, so he came back this morning. When he found out what I wanted, he got sore. Well, I'll buy me some grub and start riding. Maybe I'll have better luck when I get into Utah."

Barren lowered the paper to see Brown. It couldn't be Sam Marks. Barren didn't know how old Marks was, but with the kind of reputation he had, he'd have to be older than this fellow. He was probably just what he claimed he was, a drifter looking for a job. He wasn't even carrying a gun.

When Brown was out of sight, Barren rose and left the hotel. It had been a crazy idea anyhow. Marks had probably stayed at Wineglass and gone on. Hard to tell where he was now. Maybe hiding in the aspens watching Barren's house.

He swung into the saddle and rode out of town, but he couldn't get the stranger Brown out of his mind. The more he thought about it, the less it seemed to add up, Shortt riding into town to see a vagrant bronc buster. No, it would take more than that to bring Ben Shortt in from Wineglass.

Barren turned back and, circling, came in between Wellman's Store and the Belle Union. There he waited until Brown appeared. He was carrying a rifle, and he had a gun in a holster on his right thigh. He strode easily along the board walk to the livery stable. Presently, he rode out, tied in front of the store beside the hotel, and went in.

For the life of him, Barren could not remember ever hearing anything about Marks's appearance. That was strange, now that he thought about it. Marks had a hell of a reputation, but it was vague and mysterious.

Then it came to Barren. Sam Marks had the best disguise in the world, the appearance of youth and his bland way of making himself known as a bronc buster. No one in Starbuck would think of hooking this innocent-appearing drifter to a well-known killer like Sam Marks.

Convinced that he was right, Barren waited until Brown came out of the store with a sack of supplies that he tied behind his saddle. Barren rode into the street as Brown mounted and caught up with the man before he was out of town.

"Mind if I ride along?" Barren asked.

Brown glanced at him, a friendly grin on his face. "Free country," he said.

"I think we can do business," Barren was a little surprised to discover that he wasn't afraid. Marks might be hell hidden in the brush, but out here in the open he was just another man on a horse. "I think I'm on your list, Marks. I'm Tom Barren."

Brown's eyes showed no change of expression. He said, "Friend, you're a mite mixed up. My name's Brown. Bill Brown."

"I know," Barren said. "I mean, I looked at the hotel register and I heard the clerk talking to you, but I know you're Marks and I know Ben Shortt hired you to do a couple of killings. Maybe more. But it occurred to me that you're interested in money, so I wanted to talk to you before I got one of your slugs."

"Keep talking, mister," Marks said. "Then ride on. If you think I'm somebody else, that's your business."

"It's my business to keep from being shot," Barren said. "I'm not a rustler. Some of my neighbors are. You're called a range detective. Now I can put you onto the real rustlers, or I can top Shortt's bid to kill me. Which way do you want it?"

"Neither," Marks said. "Keep on talking till you're done."

Suddenly Barren felt uneasy. Marks was a cold fish. Too, he saw that Marks was older than he had thought at first, a fact that confirmed his conviction that the man really was Sam Marks.

"All right," Barren said. "You play a damned dirty game. The only reason you're in it is for the money. I said I would outbid Shortt. I'll pay you a thousand dollars not to kill me. I'll pay you another thousand to kill a man Shortt wants killed."

"Two thousand," Marks said in a bland voice. "That's quite a chunk of dinero." He grinned. "Just for a joke since we're lying to each other, who is the jasper you want beefed that Shortt wants out of the way, too?"

"Jeff Ardell," Barren said.

"I see." Marks nodded, his face as inscrutable as ever. "Never heard of him. Now if you're done, I'll turn off here."

Barren watched Marks swing south. Natu-

163

rally the man wouldn't admit who he was or why he was here, but he had contrived to get Barren's offer without telling Barren who he was.

Barren laughed, suddenly feeling relieved. He'd bought safety. He was sure of it, just as sure as he was sure he'd bought Jeff's death. Sam Marks wouldn't turn down another thousand dollars for killing a man Shortt was already paying for.

Barren wheeled his horse and rode back to town. He'd hear from Marks later in the day. Or maybe tonight. In any case, he'd better have the money on him when the time came.

CHAPTER XV

Jeff and Lacey Dunbar reached Dunbar's cabin in the dead, still hours of early morning. Jeff hadn't given much thought to what they would do, knowing that this situation was one they would have to play by ear, but he had assumed they would stop just long enough to pick up some grain for the horses and a sack of grub, some ammunition, and keep riding.

That was the only way to stay alive when you were bucking Sam Marks; you kept moving and circling in the hope he never had a chance to draw a bead on you, but at the same time hoping you would come up on him when he was looking in the opposite direction.

Lacey Dunbar was an expert tracker and a dead shot. Jeff was convinced that a few days of playing tag with Sam Marks would end up with Marks being on the receiving instead of the giving end of a bullet.

If Jeff had a chance to shoot Marks in the back, he'd do it with no more compunction than he'd shoot a mad dog. But there was one difficulty. A good many strangers crossed Tate Mesa during a summer, usually for personal reasons which were not subjects of conversation. Jeff had no description of the man, so he had nothing to go on if he got the drop on Marks and then the fellow denied who he was.

This line of thinking brought Jeff to a dead end. Still, there was no other way to play the game, the way Jeff saw it. He was amazed, then, when Dunbar reined up in front of his corral, dismounted, and said, "I reckon we can take care of our horses without a lantern. That bunk's going to look good to me."

"We're not staying here?" Jeff asked incredulously.

"You're damned right we are. I'm all in."

"But this is crazy," Jeff protested. "When it's daylight, Marks will smoke us down the minute we leave the cabin."

"Aw, he's probably a bad shot." Dunbar yawned. "If you're scared, keep on riding. Me, I'm about to go to sleep standing here jawing with you."

"I'm scared, all right," Jeff said, "and you ought to be."

But he swung to the ground, knowing from experience that arguing with Lacey Dunbar was a futile project. Once Dunbar made up his mind, he wouldn't budge. Too, he was probably still sore about letting Slim Tarrant go. Now he'd have his own way if it killed him.

A few minutes later they crossed the yard to the cabin, Dunbar making no effort to keep in the shadows. The moon was partly hidden by the trees to the west, but there was enough light for a man waiting in the aspens to have a good chance of hitting his target.

When they were inside, Dunbar shut and barred the door, then fumbled around finding blankets and hanging them over the windows before he lighted a lamp. Jeff sat down on the bunk and tugged off his boots. Finally he burst out, "Lacey, why in hell do you take precautions like hanging those blankets up when you know that just staying here is giving Marks an invitation to shoot us?"

"I figured it might make it a little harder for him." He sat down beside Jeff and removed his boots. "Get over next to the wall." He unbuckled his gun belt and dropped it on the floor beside the head of the bunk. "If that booger comes sneaking around, he'll get a dose of lead right in the snoot."

Jeff laid his gun belt on the floor. "I want a straight answer. I'm getting tired of your funny ones."

"So you don't think they're very funny." Dunbar laughed. "Well, I'll tell you. We handled Banjo Smith and Slim Tarrant today. When you were home, you done likewise with Buffalo Runyan. All three of 'em were genuwine hard cases, son. I don't figure Sam Marks is any tougher. Now will you go to sleep?"

A few seconds later Dunbar was snoring. Jeff tried to stay awake, to listen for sounds that might warn him of Marks's approach, and all the time he was wondering why a man as smart as Dunbar would reason in such an illogical way.

Then Jeff had the answer. Dunbar had admitted he was scared of Marks when Jeff had come Sunday night and told him. Dunbar wasn't a man to scare easily. He'd bull it through and pretend Sam Marks wasn't anything to be scared about, even if he knew he was committing suicide.

Physical exhaustion finally overcame Jeff and he dropped off to sleep. He slept until late in the afternoon, not waking until Dunbar had a fire going and coffee on the stove.

"Thought you were going to sleep all night besides all day," Dunbar said jovially.

Dunbar pulled the blankets down from the windows, pausing each time to make a careful survey of the clearing, but apparently saw nothing that alarmed him. Jeff got up, and going to a bench beside the stove, poured water into a pan and sloshed it over his face.

Whistling, Dunbar returned to the stove and started frying bacon. Jeff said, "I don't see how you can feel so good early in the morning."

Dunbar laughed. "Early in the morning! You know what time it is, son? You've been asleep twelve hours. A waste of time, that's what it is."

"I didn't sleep any twelve hours," Jeff said. "I was awake a long time thinking of that damned Marks. Lacey, tell me something. Ben Shortt wouldn't take his gun and go to Starbuck and shoot a woman or a kid. He wouldn't hold up a bank or the train or a stage coach. So why would he send for Sam Marks?"

"Sure, old Ben's good to women and dogs." Dunbar laughed and spread his hands. "Don't ask me to figure it out, but I'd guess a lot of the nabobs who hire Marks are just like Ben."

Dunbar took a pan of biscuits out of the oven, poured the coffee, and set a pot of cold beans on the table. "Ain't no banquet," he said, "but it'll satisfy my tapeworm."

Neither spoke until they finished eating. Jeff sat back and rolled a cigarette. Dunbar got up and poured a cup of coffee. He said, "Son, you know what we're going to do?"

"Wait till dark and light a shuck out of here," Jeff said.

"Still scared of Marks?" Dunbar asked tolerantly. "Well, sir, I was at first. I had the screaming heeby-jeebies, but now I'm figuring Sam Marks is just a big yarn."

Dunbar picked up his cup of coffee and drank, then put it down, hammering the table with it. "You know what I think? Old Ben never sent for Marks. He told you boys about it Sunday, knowing you'd blow up in his face. He wants you dead so he can grab the Rafter A. Maybe he wants Hank Dolan dead so he can have his wife. But what he really wanted to do was to stir things up so he could send his tough crew to Deer Creek and run everybody off."

Jeff shook his head. "That kind of thinking will get us killed."

"No it won't. I'll tell you what's happened already. Shortt had men hunting you all day yesterday. They're probably at it today.

Don't ask me why they ain't hit us here. Maybe they figured you wouldn't come here, this being the natural spot you'd come to first. The point is, so Tom Barren told me last night, that Shortt's boys had persuaded three families on the lower end of Deer Creek to pull out. A fourth one, Whitey Jackson, talked tough and they beat hell out of him. They told him they'd give him till today."

"They'll move on up the creek and hit Red O'Toole and Floyd Deems today," Jeff said. "Maybe Tom Barren."

Dunbar nodded. "Makes sense, son. Shortt told you a windy about Marks, figuring you'd tell us and we'd be ready to move by the time his crew got here with the word. Well, I ain't going. Suppose Marks is here? You don't kill a snake by cutting off his tail. You hit him just below the head, and that's what we're going to do."

He told Jeff about Barren going to Wineglass, and added, "The biggest mistake we made was not going to Wineglass Monday night. Maybe we could of got Red O'Toole to go with us. Even if we couldn't, you'n me and Tom could have done the job. Hell, Tom rode in and he rode out. Just like that."

Jeff rose and walked to the window. A rabbit hopped across the clearing, taking his own good time. A couple of chipmunks were scurrying back and forth in front of the cabin. Dunbar's pets, probably. From somewhere out in the timber a woodpecker was making a great racket.

As peaceful a scene as a man could look at, Jeff decided. Sam Marks wasn't around here now, but that didn't make Jeff believe Dunbar's theory.

Dunbar cleared the table, saying, "I hate to leave a mess, so we'll wash the dishes and skin out of here."

Jeff turned his back to the window, then, as an afterthought, moved so that he stood against the wall. He said, "This won't be easy now, getting at Wineglass. Not after Barren was there."

"That's right," Dunbar agreed amiably, "but we can do it. We'll ride in and leave our horses along the creek. Maybe we'll have to crawl on our bellies, but we'll do it if we have to. It's time old Ben found out we can hit him, too."

Jeff still didn't like it. Ben Shortt had to die, but nothing could change the fact that he was Nikki's grandfather. She hated him now, but in time she would forget that. She would remember he was her last living relative, that he had taken care of her after her folks were killed.

"I don't know, Lacey," he said. "If I have to kill Ben . . ."

"I'll do it," Dunbar said, "and spit in his face. Hell, man, think of what he's done?"

"I know, I know, but it would be something between me and Nikki. Not just now, but later on."

"Then marry some other woman. What's a woman good for? You sleep with her. She has your kids. She cooks and cleans house and all that stuff. Then, by God, if she gets uppity, take a club to her. The Indians had the right idea when they lodgepoled their squaws. Ninety-nine percent of all the trouble known to man is caused by women."

Jeff resented that. But regardless of what Dunbar thought about Nikki and women in general and marriage, Jeff refused to quarrel with him.

Dunbar would have left the country Monday morning if it hadn't been for Jeff. But he was Jeff's friend and so he had stayed.

When the dishes were washed and dried and put away neatly, Dunbar pulled on his coat and dropped two boxes of .30–30 shells into the pockets. As Dunbar picked up his rifle, Jeff said, "Lacey, let's wait till dark, then we'll light a shuck out of the country like you wanted to. You'n me will get across the Utah line and stay there until . . ."

"Oh, shut up," Dunbar said. "I ain't as big a fool as you take me for. It ain't in you to run, which same I knew all the time. You'd sneak off and leave me and try to wind this up yourself. Well, you ain't gonna do no such thing."

Dunbar walked to the door, then turned back. "Hell, chances are they'll burn me out while I'm gone. Town ain't gonna be healthy for us, so we'd better take some grub. There's a sack hanging on that nail yonder. Fill it. I'll go saddle up."

He strode out before Jeff could say anything. Irritated, Jeff did what he was told, thinking it would have been more logical for him to saddle the horses and for Dunbar to have sacked up the grub. Dunbar knew where everything was.

Jeff had to hunt for the sack which wasn't hanging on the nail as Dunbar had said. He found the biscuits and bacon without trouble, but he hesitated as he stared at the cans of food on the shelf. He didn't know which ones Dunbar wanted, or how many.

Jeff glanced outside. The light was thin. The sun had been down for some time. Jeff wished Dunbar had waited for another half hour at least . . .

A rifle shot slammed into the evening

quiet, then a second one before the echoes of the first had died. For an instant Jeff stood rooted where he was, paralyzed by the thought that Sam Marks was out there. The shots had come from the aspens on the other side of the clearing. Not from any great distance, either. In this light a man would have to be close to hit his target.

The paralysis of shock held Jeff for not more than a few seconds, then he grabbed his Winchester from where it leaned against the wall by the door and ran outside. He knew what he would find before he reached the corral; he had a sudden, terrifying feeling he had known all the time this was what would happen.

Lacey Dunbar lay in the dust in front of the corral gate. Jeff knelt beside him. Dunbar was dead. One slug had ripped through his chest and would have killed him without the second which must have been fired as he was falling.

Kneeling here in the dust beside the body of the man who had been his best friend as long as he could remember, Jeff wanted to cry and couldn't; he tried to swallow and couldn't. Now the truth came to him. Lacey Dunbar had told Jeff to sack up the grub because he knew that if Sam Marks was waiting out there in the aspens, he'd get the first man who left the cabin.

Then the fury hit Jeff like the crackling rush of lightning. Marks would be gone by now. In the dusk light Jeff would never be able to track him. But that didn't seem important. Lacey Dunbar's words raced through his mind: *You don't kill a snake by cutting off his tail.*

Jeff rose. He shook his fist at the aspens where Marks had hidden, but he wasn't thinking of Marks. He shouted, "I'm going to kill you, Ben. God damn you, I'm going to kill you."

He picked Dunbar's body up and carrying him to the cabin, laid him on the bunk and went out. He closed the door, crossed to the corral and saddled his horse. Slipping the Winchester into the boot, he mounted and rode east toward Tom Barren's ranch. He would pick Barren up if Barren wanted to go. If not, he would go alone.

The thought that Ben Shortt was Nikki's grandfather didn't even occur to Jeff. It wouldn't have seemed important if it had.

Chapter XVI

Matthew Ardell woke shortly after dawn Wednesday morning. He couldn't seem to sleep much these days. Not that he was in pain. It was just that his mind was as active as ever, but his body made him an invalid. So, sentenced to his bed or the wheel chair, unable to do the things that only Matthew Ardell was qualified to do, his frustration had grown until he thought he could not retain his sanity for another day.

He felt of his thin, useless legs, then Nancy stirred beside him, her back to him. Gently so he wouldn't waken her, he laid a hand on her hip. When he had been a whole man, this had been enough to arouse him. She had been a lusty woman, unashamed of the fact that she enjoyed being Matthew Ardell's wife.

This hurt more than anything else. As long as he lived, she would not be able to marry again, and he was terrified by the prospect of living for years, more vegetable than man. On the other hand, he was even more terrified by the fear that he would die and she would marry Tom Barren.

Barren pretended to be his friend, and Matthew pretended that he thought Barren was his friend, but he knew better. He had always been a good judge of human nature, and for years he had sensed a basic dishonesty in Tom Barren.

He had seen Barren look at Nancy and had known what was in his mind, but it was not a thing he could talk about to Nancy. Being the kind of woman she was, she did not understand Barren and therefore did not see through him. She considered him a friend and a neighbor, so she would turn to him if Matthew died.

Well then, he just wouldn't die, Matthew decided, and felt like laughing at himself. A man was pretty far gone when he took upon himself the decision of when he would die.

Presently Nancy stirred and turning to face him, smiled. If she slept well, she always woke this way, not wanting to get up and for the moment being lazily content. She kissed him and patted him on the chest, carefully keeping her hands away from his legs because she knew how sympathy of any kind hurt him.

"It's nice to have Nikki here," Nancy said. "If I could have picked out Jeff's wife, I mean, a dream girl, it would have been Nikki."

Matthew smiled, for Nancy was always having dreams and always believing in them. Before either knew of Jeff's interest in Nikki, Nancy had told Matthew one morning about the girl Jeff would marry. She had seen her in a dream and described her. Thinking about it, Matthew remembered that the girl Nancy had described had not resembled Nikki at all.

"She's fine," Matthew said. "Real fine."

Nancy yawned and got up and dressed. Matthew watched her until she left the room. He listened to her start the fire in the kitchen, then followed her movements as she went outside, letting the screen door bang behind her. She chopped enough wood to last through the morning, then she came in and dropped an armload into the box beside the stove. When Jeff was gone Nancy had to chop wood, one of the many things that added weight to Matthew's sense of futility.

When breakfast was ready, Nancy came to the bedroom and helped Matthew dress. Then she wheeled him into the kitchen. He could handle the chair reasonably well, but usually Nancy or Jeff pushed when either was around.

If Nancy was worried about what might happen today, she didn't show it. She was as cheerful as ever, sometimes speaking tartly which was her way and didn't mean anything. Thinking back over their years together when he had been a whole man, he knew he had been lucky. He hoped Nikki would be as good a wife to Jeff as Nancy had been to him.

Suddenly Matthew remembered that he had left his revolver under his pillow in bed. Jeff would give him hell if he were here. Justifiably so, too. Sooner or later the Wineglass men would come, and when they did, that gun was the only defense he had. He had been a good shot before his accident. At close quarters he could still hit his target.

Nancy went outside. And as soon as she was gone, Matthew wheeled into the bedroom and lifted the gun from under his pillow. He thought about this a minute, not wanting to worry Nancy or even let her know he had the gun. Finally he pulled the top quilt from the bed and spread it over his lap, covering the gun. He was surprised at himself, especially at his certainty he would use the Colt if he had to.

He rolled himself through the front room and out on the porch where he spent the morning. He loved the view from here, the La Sals on his right, the San Juans to the left, and The Lookout straight in front of him across the mesa, a single, conelike peak that poked skyward from the long ridges that formed a wavy line against the blue sky.

But this morning he was in no mood to enjoy beauty. He kept thinking about Ben Shortt, and asking himself what would possess a man of his age to go crazy, which was the only way Matthew could explain Shortt's actions. But explanations did no good. You had to face the reality of facts.

Matthew had honestly believed a man could avoid violence, by one means or another, a belief that had been destroyed last night. Ben Shortt had sent Buffalo Runyan here to kill Jeff. He would have done it if Jeff hadn't killed him, and then he would have taken Nikki back to Wineglass.

That was the reason Matthew was certain they would have more trouble today. When Runyan failed to return to Wineglass and Slim Tarrant got back from the Halfway House, Ben Shortt would do something. The pattern of violence had been set. Now it would be followed to the bitter end.

He heard talk from the kitchen and knew

that Nikki was up. Presently she came out of the house and sat down on the top step. She said, "I wanted to make a good impression on Jeff's folks the first day I'm with them, then I sleep until noon. I'm apologizing, Mr. Ardell. I'm not really lazy."

He smiled at her. "You've already made a good impression. We know how tired you were, so don't worry about it."

Nancy ran into the front room from the kitchen, calling, "Matthew, two men on horses are close to the rim. They're just staring over here and not moving."

"Wheel me into the kitchen," he said.

Nikki jumped up and ran to the back door. Nancy rolled Matthew's chair into the kitchen. Nikki was standing on the porch. She said, "It's too far to be sure, but I think it's Slim Tarrant and Curly Jones."

"They're about where Lacey Dunbar and Jeff split up," Matthew said. "Get Nikki into the cave." His right hand slipped under the quilt and gripped the walnut butt of the revolver. "The only way they'll whip us is to burn the house."

"They wouldn't do that," Nancy said. "They'll look around, and when they don't find Nikki, they'll go the other way."

"You don't know them," Nikki said. "Curly Jones is a wolf. I think there have been times when Grandpa's wished he'd never hired him."

Nancy tugged at the girl's arm. "Come on. You've got to hide."

Nikki shook her head. "Jeff left Runyan's gun. Let me go into the bedroom. If they start trouble, I'll use the gun."

"That's my job." Matthew showed them the Peacemaker. "Go into the cave. It isn't comfortable, but you can stand it."

Nancy stared at the gun in Matthew's hand, shocked. She hadn't been surprised when she had seen the quilt on his lap because he chilled even on hot days, but the gun was the last thing she expected to see.

"I know, Nancy," Matthew said, "but there are times in a man's life when he has to do things he doesn't want to. Maybe doesn't even believe in. This is such a time." He jerked his head at the front room. "Go on, Nikki."

She obeyed, Nancy following. Matthew rolled his chair behind them. Nancy moved the rug that covered most of the front room floor, lifted a trap door, and motioned for Nikki to go down the ladder.

"It's dark and it'll smell musty," Nancy said, "but you'll be safer there."

"I'll be all right," Nikki said.

She disappeared down the ladder. Nancy

lowered the door into place and covered it with the rug. Matthew moved his chair until it was directly over the trap door. Nancy came to him and laid a hand on his shoulder.

"It can't be this bad," she whispered. "Bad enough for you to have a gun. They'll kill us, Matthew, if you try to shoot them."

"Not if I kill them first," he said. "This is something we don't understand. I wouldn't have believed it a few days ago if Jeff had told me, but after what happened last night, and what happened at the Halfway House, I can believe anything."

"But I'm a woman," Nancy cried, "and you're a . . . a . . ."

"An invalid," he said. "A fraction of a man. You might as well say it, Nancy. I know what I am. I know what people say. I know what it has cost you to live with me the last three years."

"Matthew, Matthew, I didn't mean . . ."

"Of course, you didn't, but it's the truth. Now you go back and watch them. If they're coming, I want to know it."

She hesitated, her face so pale it alarmed him. Then she whispered, "I'm sorry, Matthew. But please believe me when I say it hasn't cost me anything to live with you."

She turned away and went back into the

kitchen. She called, "They're going the other way."

"Watch them," he said. "It may be a trick."

She remained there ten minutes, then came back through the house. "They're gone," she said. "They rode southwest."

"They'll be back," Matthew said, and moved his chair off the rug. "Get Nikki up."

But Nancy didn't move. She said, "Matthew, it just doesn't make any sense that those men would hurt us. We can't hurt them."

"I told you it's something we don't understand. It doesn't make sense for Ben to send for Sam Marks. Or to have Buffalo Runyan try to kill Jeff. But I guess many things that I did never made sense to Ben Shortt." He hesitated, and added, "Not even to Jeff." He motioned at the trap door. "Get her up."

Nancy lifted the trap door, calling, "They went the other way, Nikki."

She climbed the ladder, wiping cobwebs from her face. She asked Matthew, "You think that's all there is to it?"

"I wish I could say yes," he told her, "but I can't. They'll be back."

Nancy replaced the trap door and pulled the rug into place. "I'll get dinner."

The afternoon passed slowly. Afternoons always dragged for Matthew. He read if he had anything to read. Sometimes he slept. But today he didn't feel like reading. He couldn't run the risk of sleeping, so he remained on the front porch.

Then, in late afternoon, they came again, riding up out of an arroyo southwest of the Rafter A. They took a line directly for the house, and even at this distance, it seemed to him there was a predatory air about them. He smiled, surprised that he could laugh at himself. He was imagining things simply because he knew they were predatory men.

Nancy was back in the kitchen starting supper. Matthew called, "They're coming. Get Nikki back into the cave."

He heard talk between the two women, Nancy begging and Nikki arguing, but in the end Nikki obeyed and went into the cave. Matthew rolled his chair into the house. Nancy picked up some sewing and pulled her rocking chair over the trap door.

She looked at Matthew, trying to smile. "They'll come in and ask about Nikki. Maybe look around, then they'll ride off."

She was living in her dream world again, he thought. Well, let her live in it as long as she could. It wouldn't last for more than a minute. He examined the gun. Five loads. They would have to do. He'd have no time to reload.

He would take Curly Jones first. If Nikki was right, Jones was the more dangerous of the two. Matthew cocked the gun, holding it in his right hand, and with his left pulled the quilt back over the gun.

From where he sat next to a window, he watched them ride up and dismount, then stand talking for a minute or more. Why didn't they get it over with?

Suddenly he realized his pulse was pounding, that sweat was dribbling down his forehead. He looked at Nancy who was sewing, apparently unconcerned. He wondered how he looked. Well, he didn't care. It was all the better if he looked scared. They would expect no trouble from him.

Both men walked to the barn. They were gone for fifteen or twenty minutes, probably making a close inspection of the outbuildings. Having made certain Nikki wasn't out there, they strode toward the house.

They stepped up on the porch and walked in without knocking. Tarrant's face still held the marks of Jeff's fists. He cuffed back his hat, looking at Nancy and completely ignoring Matthew.

"Last night your son Jeff and Lacey Dunbar kidnapped Nikki Shortt," Tarrant said. "We trailed them to the rim, then their tracks separated. Suppose you tell us where the girl is."

"Jeff was here last night," Nancy said. "Lacey must have taken Nikki with him. We haven't seen her."

"You're lying," Tarrant said. "We're taking her to Wineglass. It will save you trouble if you tell us where she is."

Nancy kept rocking. "You can look around, but you won't find her. You're not welcome, you know. We didn't invite you into our house."

Tarrant grinned. "No, you didn't for a fact." He jerked his head at Jones. "Look around, Curly. They've got her hidden right here under our noses, but they'll tell us, all right."

Jones disappeared into the kitchen. Tarrant walked to the walnut stand and picked up Runyan's gun. "Buffalo Runyan's horse came in last night. This is Runyan's gun. Where is he?"

"I don't know," Nancy said. "All I can tell you is that Jeff shot him last night, but I don't know what he did with the body."

Anger was stirring in Matthew. Both Tarrant and Jones had ignored him from the time they had come into the house.

"Well now," Tarrant said, "I guess that's enough to hang Jeff."

"It wasn't murder if that's what you're trying to make out," Nancy said spiritedly. "Runyan tried to kill Jeff."

"You're lying again," Tarrant said, sliding the gun under his waistband. "Find anything, Curly?"

Jones had come back into the room. "No, but there's some clothes in the other bedroom that looks like hers."

Tarrant strode to where Nancy sat. "You've got ten seconds to tell us where she is. No more. If you don't, you'll get a hell of a beating. You'll wind up telling us, so you might as well tell us now and keep from getting hurt."

"Don't touch her," Matthew said, and didn't recognize his own voice, high and strained.

Tarrant and Jones still ignored him. Nancy stared at Tarrant as if she thought he didn't mean it. "You wouldn't come into our house and beat me," she said. "A woman?"

"All right, we'll give it to the old man," Tarrant said. "So you'd better tell us. We're not leaving here without the girl."

"No," Jones said. "We'll work Mrs. Ardell over, then the old man will tell."

Tarrant shrugged. He said, "All right," and stepped back. "You've had your ten seconds."

189

Nancy started to get up and fell back into the chair, her legs unable to hold her weight. She still didn't believe they'd do it, Matthew thought, but he knew they would. He'd known it from the first. But he hadn't thought they'd be as indifferent as they were, as if it were a simple ranch chore like branding calves.

Jones moved toward Nancy. "How about it?"

"No," she screamed. "Get out of here."

Jones hit her on the side of the face, sending her sprawling out of her chair to the floor. Matthew heard her moan, heard Tarrant say, "Now, by God, you'll tell us or nobody will recognize your face again."

Matthew was cool. He wasn't even trembling. He had only one regret, that he hadn't killed them sooner and saved Nancy the pain of the blow. With his left hand he threw back the quilt. Lining his gun on Jones, he shot him through the heart.

Tarrant wheeled and grabbed for his gun. He never got it clear of leather. Matthew shot him twice, once in the head and once in the body as he fell. Matthew was surprised that he felt no more guilt than if he had shot two mad dogs, which was what these men were.

"Get Nikki up here," he said to Nancy

190

who was on her knees, a hand raised to the side of her face where Jones had struck her. "We can't get rid of the bodies, so we won't stay here. You and Nikki will have to harness the team to the wagon right away."

He laid the gun on his lap, staring at Tarrant's body, then he said, "I wish it had been Ben."

CHAPTER XVII

By the time Jeff reached Deer Creek above Tom Barren's ranch, the last trace of color had left the western horizon. The moon would not be up yet for some time, so the only light was from the stars. Even the star-shine was blotted out here in the thick-growing aspens. Jeff, sitting his saddle at the upper edge of the meadows, could not make out Barren's buildings that lay below him.

Jeff dismounted, leaving his reins dragging. For several minutes he stood there, watching and listening. He could see nothing, and the only things he heard were the natural sounds he would hear any night: an owl hooting, a coyote barking from the mesa, the steady whispering of the water in the creek.

The first crazy fury had died in Jeff; the grief hadn't. He wondered if it ever would. He had often been irritated by Dunbar's facetious remarks, by his laughing at things which shouldn't have been laughed at, by his lack of understanding of Jeff's love for Nikki.

But none of those things had been important. Now that Dunbar was gone, Jeff knew he could miss him as he had never dreamed he would miss anyone. It seemed strange he hadn't understood that when Dunbar was alive, yet that was the natural way of life.

Strange, too, that Jeff did not feel the hatred for Sam Marks that he had thought he would. Ben Shortt was the man he hated; Ben Shortt was the one who had killed Lacey Dunbar just as surely as if he had pulled the trigger instead of Sam Marks. Shortt was probably sitting at home waiting to hear from Marks, and Marks might be standing within ten feet of Jeff right now.

Jeff had not tried to track Marks after Dunbar's killing. The man had run the instant he'd fired the fatal shots, or he'd have got Jeff when he came out of the cabin. With darkness coming on, Jeff knew he couldn't follow Marks's trail. He would blunder into an ambush if he tried, and Jeff Ardell wanted to stay alive.

But these were minor points that had occurred to him. The controlling fact that dictated his action was the knowledge that killing Sam Marks would not change the future. Shortt's death would.

Now the question was how to locate Barren. If he was in the house and Jeff walked up to it, he'd probably get shot before Barren found out who he was. It would likely be the same if Barren was sleeping out here in the aspens and Jeff stumbled onto him.

The safest thing he could do was to ride on without Barren. But he lingered because he wanted to tell Barren about Dunbar. He still didn't know what to do, for he was fully aware that if Marks was hiding near here, Jeff would bring the killer down on him the instant he called to Barren.

Jeff finally decided he'd have to go on. As he reluctantly turned to his horse, a man asked, "That you, Jeff?"

Jeff's movement was instinctive. He spun away from his horse and dropped, drawing his gun as he fell. When he was belly flat on the ground, he realized it was Barren who had spoken. He said shakily, "Yeah, this is Jeff. What the hell, Tom? You'll get yourself killed doing stunts like this."

"No," Barren said. "I'm hugging the ground behind an aspen. If you had cut loose, I wouldn't have got hit."

Jeff rose and holstered his gun. He said, "I wanted to see you, but I couldn't figure out how to let you know I was here."

"That's what's been worrying me." Barren laughed nervously. "I heard you, but it's so dark I couldn't make you out. I figured it must be you, riding in from Dunbar's place. Where's Lacey?"

"Dead," Jeff answered, and told him what had happened.

Barren cursed, then added in a strained voice, "It's their turn now. Lacey said you got Banjo Smith."

"And Buffalo Runyan," Jeff said, and told him about the fight at the Rafter A.

"Two on each side," Barren said bitterly. "Whitey Jackson died from the beating they gave him."

"One for Sam Marks and one for the Wineglass crew," Jeff said, "and both for Ben Shortt."

"Old Ben's almost finished what he started out to do," Barren said. "I saw Red O'Toole this afternoon. Everybody below him is gone. Whitey's death persuaded them."

"You wanted to go after Shortt Monday," Jeff said. "I wish we'd done it. I wish I'd killed him Sunday. And I wished you'd got him when you were there."

"Wishing doesn't do much good now," Barren muttered.

"Tells us what's got to be done," Jeff said. "This afternoon Lacey said you don't kill a snake by cutting off its tail. I'm going after the head. I figured you'd want to go."

"No, I'm staying here," Barren said. "If Shortt's men try to burn me out like they did some of the others, they'll have a fight."

Jeff had not expected this from Barren, but he didn't argue. He said, "All right, Tom," and turned to his horse.

"Don't get your hackles up," Barren snapped. "If we'd gone after Ben Monday night, we could have wiped Wineglass off the map. Lacey was alive. O'Toole would have gone with us. Now there's just us. And another thing. Shortt will have guards out after me getting to him the way I did. It'd be suicide, Jeff."

Jeff rode toward the creek, making no effort to answer Barren's arguments. Suicide or not, it was the only thing he could do. As he climbed to the mesa, he asked himself why Tom Barren had refused to go with him. Then he remembered Dunbar saying that no one really understood Barren.

Reaching the top, Jeff struck out northeast toward Wineglass. He glanced at the stars, figuring the time and wondering if he could reach Wineglass before the moon came up. By now Shortt knew he was in a fight. He'd have a guard out, maybe more than one. Barren might have been right in saying this was suicide.

Jeff rode as fast as he could in the darkness, taking a straight course across the mesa and watching the eastern sky for the first sign of the moon. Then he heard a wagon off to the north. He reined up, puzzled.

Shortt wouldn't send men out in a wagon. It wouldn't be one of the Deer Creek families. Most of them were gone. He thought of his parents and Nikki, but that seemed an absurd notion. His father hadn't been off the ranch since his accident.

Jeff turned north toward the wagon, thinking that if it was his folks and Nikki, they must have had a compelling reason to leave the Rafter A. If the Wineglass men had come and taken Nikki, and Shortt had her now, Jeff's plans would have to be changed.

He dropped into an arroyo, aware that this was costing him time he couldn't afford to lose, but he couldn't think of any way to avoid it. If, by some crazy twist of Shortt's thinking, this was a Wineglass wagon filled with Wineglass men, or some of Steve Lawrence's boys, they'd cut him down the instant they recognized him.

So he waited, hearing the wagon grind closer, then his mother's voice came to him clearly, "Things don't look right at night,

Matthew. I don't know if we're lost or not."

Jeff rode out of the arroyo, calling, "Ma, it's me, Jeff."

The wagon stopped. Nikki cried out, an incoherent sound of sheer relief. She jumped down from the seat and ran toward him. A moment later he was out of the saddle and she was in his arms, her hands gripping him fiercely, then she lifted them to his head, caressing him, and tipped her face back for his kiss.

"Jeff," his mother called, "what are you doing out here?"

Nikki drew back. She said, choking and swallowing so that the words came in bursts and he caught only part of them, "Tarrant and Jones came to get me. Your father shot both of them."

They walked toward the wagon, Jeff leading his horse. He found it hard to believe that his father could have killed two men. Then he reached the wagon and put a hand up toward his mother. She took it and squeezed it, asking, "Are you all right?"

"Sure I am." He turned and held out his hand to his father who lay on a mattress in the wagon bed. "Nikki says you stomped a couple of snakes."

"That's just what they were," Matthew said. "I told you I'd look out for Nikki."

"I'm proud of you," Jeff said.

"I'm a little proud of myself," Matthew said. "I guess that when the time comes, a man can do what has to be done. I figured Ben would send somebody to find Tarrant and Jones when they didn't get back, so I knew we couldn't stay there."

"We're going to Tom Barren's ranch," Nancy said. "Matthew wanted to go to town, but I didn't. Seems to me everybody in town is afraid of Ben Shortt."

"Almost everybody," Jeff agreed.

Miles Rebus was the one exception, but he couldn't hide three people. Again Jeff had the agonizing experience of having to make a choice where there was no choice just as he had when he'd taken Nikki to the Rafter A. Tom Barren's ranch wasn't safe, but it was as safe as any place.

"Are we headed right?" Matthew asked.

"Keep going," Jeff said. "Bear a little more to the west. I'm going to Wineglass. I'll be at Tom's place before sunup."

Nikki's fingers squeezed his arm. "Are you trying to get killed?"

"No, but I've got to go." He told them about Dunbar, adding, "Ben Shortt is going to pay for Lacey's killing, Nikki. Sam Marks later, but first it's got to be Shortt."

He put his arm around her and hugged

her. She said, "I won't beg for Grandpa's life, Jeff. Not after all that has happened, but I will beg for yours."

"I'll be back." He kissed her and helped her back into the wagon seat. "Don't worry about me."

He strode to his horse, knowing that he had taken too much time. The wagon was moving again. He rode on, and presently the lights in the windows of the Wineglass buildings came into view, were pinpoints across the grass.

If Lacey Dunbar was riding beside him . . . But that was foolish thinking. He was alone. Nothing could change that now.

Chapter XVIII

When Jeff reached the county road, he turned to circle the horse pasture that lay south of the Wineglass buildings. The one chance he had to get out alive was to sneak in and get out quick, so he took the long way around.

The moon was showing a yellow rind above the eastern horizon when Jeff reached Lookout Creek which headed in the high country to the south, flowed through town, and making a bend, came within fifty yards of the rear of the Wineglass ranch house.

Jeff was relieved when he reached the creek and turned north to ride close to the willows which made a thick screen along the banks. By keeping to the shadows of the willows, he was less likely to be seen than when he was riding across the mesa in the moonlight.

He dismounted directly back of the house and stood motionless, listening and hearing nothing except the rush of the water behind him and an occasional laugh from the bunkhouse. He couldn't see anything moving, yet he had a feeling that someone was close.

Once he jumped and turned, his hand on his gun butt, thinking he had heard a dry willow branch break under a man's boot. He couldn't see anything and the sound was not repeated, so he decided it was his imagination.

He had expected to find a guard somewhere around the house, but he could neither see nor hear anyone. The bunkhouse was full of Wineglass hands. Some of Steve Lawrence's Triangle men might be here, too. If there was a guard he had to get rid of him without attracting the attention of the men in the bunkhouse.

He had told himself he had to sneak in and get out quick, but now he saw that his reasoning had been superficial. The only way he could kill Shortt was to face him with a gun and let Shortt have a chance at his own weapon, but the instant a shot was fired, men would come boiling out of the bunkhouse.

Well, he was here and he wasn't turning back. He mentally cursed Tom Barren for coming here Monday night for apparently no purpose except to tweak Ben Shortt's nose. Jeff's job would be easier if Barren had never made that visit.

He ran toward a shed that stood between him and the rear of the house. He was in the open for thirty yards, the moon high enough so that anyone who was watching would see him. He made it, expecting a gun to open up any instant. But it didn't. He hugged the wall of the shed until he caught his breath.

Again he had the haunting feeling that somebody was in the willows not far from his horse, but he couldn't see anyone. He eased around the shed and stopped again, staring at the back door. He considered trying to get into the house through that door. He gave it up, even though all the lights were in the front. Never having been in the rear half of the house, he would bump into something in the darkness and alarm Shortt, thus losing the advantage of surprise.

The only thing to do was to ease around the side to the front. Shortt was probably in his office. What Jeff did after that would depend on what happened. He thought briefly of Nikki, knowing he had never wanted to live as much as he did now. But Lacey Dunbar had wanted to live, too.

Jeff took a step away from the shed and

leaped back. A man paced casually around the house, a rifle in one hand, the glow of his cigar a red coal as he drew on it. He sat down on a back step for a minute or two, took the cigar out of his mouth, and then got up and walked toward the shed.

Jeff's first thought was that the man had seen him or heard him and was coming to investigate. Then he saw he was wrong. The guard came halfway to the shed and kicked at a chunk, probably bored by the whole business.

The man put the cigar back into his mouth, but it had gone cold. He struck a match, the flame lighting his face. Jeff recognized him, another one of Shortt's hard cases named Mick Hennessy.

When Hennessy had his cigar going, he turned toward the house. Jeff caught him in three long strides. Hennessy started to whirl, but he was too slow. Jeff slapped his right hand over Hennessy's mouth and brought his left arm under his chin hard against his throat, cutting off his wind.

Hennessy made a gurgling noise, but Jeff was the stronger man, and in spite of Hennessy's plunging, he was unable to break free. Jeff pulled his gun and slammed the barrel across the top of Hennessy's head. He sagged and went limp.

Jeff dragged the man back into the shadow of the shed and tossed the rifle into the weeds, then he sprinted toward the house and along the side to the front. He stopped at the corner and glanced toward the bunkhouse. A man stepped outside, the lamp light behind him so that his shadow fell ahead of him into the yard. It was Steve Lawrence.

Jeff wondered if they had found Slim Tarrant and Curly Jones yet. Tarrant had been Shortt's key man. Now that he was gone, Lawrence would probably give the orders. A mousey man, but dangerous enough with a crew of toughs behind him.

"Wonder where Mick is?" Lawrence said.

"Probably asleep," a man inside the bunkhouse said irritably. "Come on back here, Steve. You can't keep being lucky."

Lawrence went back in and the flow of loud talk went on. Quickly Jeff crossed to the front door that was open and slipped into the house. Time was running against him, he thought. If Hennessy was supposed to show up at the bunkhouse occasionally, they'd miss him and start looking.

Jeff catfooted along the hall to the door that opened into the front room. From where he stood, he could not see Shortt, but there was a light in the office, so Jeff was reasonably sure the old man was there.

Jeff listened, but hearing no one else in the house, he crossed the front room. He was within two steps of the office door when a floor board squealed under his feet. Gun in his hand, he took two long strides that carried him into the office and brought him face to face with Ben Shortt.

The old cowman was working on his books. He looked up, scowling at what he probably supposed was an interruption from one of his men. Whatever his thoughts were, he was plainly jolted when he saw who it was. He had the expression of a man whose mind had gone completely blank.

Jeff slid into the room, his back to the wall, then it occurred to him that if any of the crew walked past the front of the house, they could see him, so he moved toward the window and stood beside it, his back still to the wall.

"You can pay Sam Marks for his first murder," Jeff said. "Lacey Dunbar got it late this afternoon."

Shortt said nothing. He sat with both hands on the desk, his face gray. The corners of his mouth began to twitch. At this moment he looked every one of his seventy years.

"Where is Marks?" Jeff asked.

Shortt swallowed, then he said with an effort, "I don't know." He swallowed again, and asked, "Where's Nikki?"

"Tarrant and Jones went after her, but they won't bring her back," Jeff said. "They're dead. I asked you where Marks is."

"I don't know," Shortt answered. "I told you."

"It doesn't make any difference," Jeff said. "I'll find him, but right now it's you I'm after." Jeff holstered his gun. "Get up, Ben. I'm giving you a chance for your iron. That's more than Marks does."

Shortt shook his head. "To hell with you. You'll never get out of here alive."

Jeff said, "I'll let you have it where you sit if I have to, but I'd never hire a dry gulcher like Sam Marks to murder a man from the brush. I'd give a man a chance. I'm giving you yours now unless you want to die like Lacey did."

Shortt acted as if he were going to get up, shoulders tense, hands pressed palm down against the top of his desk. Then he went slack, head tipping forward. "By God, Jeff, you've got sand in your craw, coming here like this. Too bad you didn't stick with me."

"Make your play," Jeff said. "I've run out

of time."

He heard someone coming across the front room. Shortt grinned. He said, "You have for a fact."

Jeff drew his gun, waiting for the man in the other room to come in. A moment later Hank Dolan stepped through the door, closing it behind him. Dolan was the last man Jeff expected to see, and when he glanced at Shortt, he saw that the old man was more surprised than he was.

"Don't point your gun at me, Jeff," Dolan said. "I'm on your side. I've been as close as the creek two different times aiming to come in and shoot this old bastard, but both times I lost my nerve. Tonight I followed you in. When I saw who it was, I figured that if you had enough grit to try it, I did, too."

Jeff wasn't sure Dolan was telling the truth, but he remembered thinking that someone had been out there in the willows behind him. Apparently it had been Dolan. If he had been playing Shortt's game, he would have shot Jeff in the back.

Dolan was scared enough to be trembling, but there was a haunted look on the man's thin face that Jeff had never seen before. Worked up as he was, Dolan was capable of anything.

"I gave Ben a chance for his gun," Jeff said, "but he wants to take it like a sitting duck."

"He's my meat," Dolan said. "What kind of hell do you think I've lived in all these years?" He motioned with a shaky hand. "Get out of here, boy. I'll take care of this son of a bitch, but before I do, I'm going to tell him why I'm doing it."

"No," Jeff said. "I don't trust you, Hank. You sucked around after Ben too long."

"I quit sucking the day you jumped the traces," Dolan said hoarsely. "Last Sunday. If you had a wife who . . ." He stopped. "Jeff, go out through that window while you can."

They glared at each other, Jeff still not sure of Dolan. There was this one short moment when Jeff's attention was fixed on Dolan, not Shortt, a moment long enough for Shortt to come up out of his chair and blow out the lamp on his desk.

Jeff fired twice at where he thought Shortt would be. Shortt threw a shot that missed, and Jeff saw that Shortt had moved to one side. Jeff fired again at Shortt's new position, not sure whether he had hit the man or not.

"Get out through the window," Dolan yelled.

Jeff knew he had to move, but to go through the window and cross the front of the house with its lighted windows was certain death. He opened the door into the front room and raced toward the back. He heard men pound toward the house, some of them yelling, then Dolan's shout, "It's Ardell. He just shot and killed Ben. Down the lane, Steve. His horse is out there."

Jeff ran through the back door, thinking that if Dolan had moved his horse, he was a goner. He heard more yelling, and Lawrence's bellowed order, "Saddle up. I'll give a thousand dollars to the man who catches that bastard."

Then Jeff was past the shed. He saw his horse and took the first good breath he'd drawn since Shortt blew the lamp out. He'd bungled it, he told himself as he swung into the saddle. But as he dug in the steel, he wasn't sure. Dolan might have told the truth when he'd yelled that Jeff had shot and killed Shortt. But whether he had or not, Jeff couldn't wait to find out.

He struck off south, his horse in a dead run. He heard men's voices raised behind him. One of the men yelled, "There he goes. By the creek."

They'd be on his tail and he knew he'd played it foolish. If he'd crossed the creek

210

and taken it easy, they wouldn't have spotted him. Now he was riding for his life.

Chapter XIX

The night suddenly became alive with Wineglass riders. Some were west of him on the county road that led to Starbuck. Those were the ones who worried Jeff. Apparently they had been the first to saddle up and had taken Dolan's word that Jeff was headed down the lane toward the road.

There was only the width of the horse pasture between Jeff and the men on the county road. If he turned west at the end of the pasture, he'd run into them.

Any way he figured it, Jeff was cut off from Deer Creek. So he continued to ride south. The men behind him weren't gaining, but he wasn't throwing them off, either. Starbuck was directly ahead of him, only a few lights showing at this hour.

At least a dozen men after him, too many to fight. They were too close for him to circle back, a good trick if the country was rough enough to hide him while the pursuit roared past. But the land was level here with no arroyos to drop into. Even the willows along the creek had been cleared and the bank wasn't more than two feet high.

He couldn't keep this pace. He'd kill his horse, or the animal would fall and throw him, and the Wineglass men would be on top of him before he could make a run for it. The one chance he had was to hide in town. The only man in Starbuck who would help him was Miles Rebus, and Miles would get into trouble if he did. He might be in trouble anyway. His house would be the first place the Wineglass men would search.

When Jeff reached town, he swung right, knowing he had only a minute or two before the Wineglass riders arrived. Because he couldn't think of a better place, he turned into the lumberyard.

He swung down and, taking his Winchester, left his horse between two piles of lumber. He ran into the alley that paralleled Main Street and raced east toward Miles Rebus' house. He'd take the preacher's horse, he thought, and try to get out of town while his pursuers were fanning out searching for him.

He could have dived into any of a dozen sheds and barns along the alley, but if they found him and cornered him, he was a

213

goner. He had his tail in a crack now. Even if he stole a fresh horse, he had little chance of slipping out of town. With the moon as bright as it was, the odds were a hundred to one they'd spot him.

He was at the east end of the business block when the Wineglass men reached the lumberyard. One of them found his horse and gave a yell. Steve Lawrence shouted, "He ain't had time to go far. He's hiding around here. Or headed down the alley. Riley, you and Brogan take a look down there. Stilly, you and Quinn go to the preacher's house."

Jeff had been able to keep in the shadow along the side of the alley, but he was in the open now, with a scattering of houses here on the east side of town. Miles Rebus' house was the last one, a block or more beyond where Jeff was now. He heard horses in the alley behind him and others in the street, likely Stilly's and Quinn's. He had only seconds left before they'd be on him.

For a terrifying moment he thought he was whipped. If he stayed where he was they'd see him. The only thing he could think of was the irrigation ditch which brought water into town for lawns and gardens. He dropped into it and lay belly flat, the weeds on both sides tall enough to hide him.

He was thankful the water wasn't in the ditch yet. It would be in a day or two, as dry as it had been. He heard Stilly and Quinn ride past along the street; he heard the two men Lawrence had told to have a look along the alley coming toward him.

One of them, he thought it was Brogan's voice, said in a worried tone, "Hell, I hope we don't find him. He'll blow our heads off before we know we've found him."

"He'll give himself away," the other said, "and we'll have him."

"That'll sure help the gent who gets his head blowed off," the first man said sourly. "I suppose you want me to take the lead."

They weren't making much of a search. Now Jeff realized he would have been better off to have hidden in one of the sheds. Unless Lawrence got lanterns and insisted on a careful hunt, a man hiding in a hay mow or granary would be safe until morning.

The shouting had wakened some of the townspeople and lamps were coming to life in several of the houses. One of the men in the alley said, "Young Ardell turned out to be hell on high, red wheels. It'd be safer to poke a rattlesnake with a stick than to dig him out of one of them sheds."

They stood talking for a minute, then they

215

turned back. He began to crawl. The ditch would take him to the rear of Miles Rebus' house. He had to keep crawling until he got there whether he took Miles' horse or not. The preacher was going to need help.

Stilly was a bad one, a hard case about the same caliber of Banjo Smith and Curly Jones. Quinn wasn't. He was an old hand who had worked for Ben Shortt as long as Jeff could remember. He was loyal to Shortt, though, so at a time like this, he'd be hard on Miles if he thought the preacher was hiding Jeff.

Jeff was past the first house when the back door opened, lamp light falling beyond the man who stood in the doorway, his shadow long and grotesque against the packed dirt of the yard. Jeff dropped flat, feeling an impulse to sneeze and somehow stifling it. Horses pounded along the alley. The man in the doorway called, "What's going on?"

"We're hunting Jeff Ardell," Lawrence answered. "He shot and killed Ben Shortt tonight."

"The hell," the man said, and quickly closed the door.

The riders went on, Lawrence shouting, "Stilly! Find him?"

So Ben Shortt was really dead! Now Steve Lawrence was tough, Jeff thought, real tough while he was hunting Shortt's killer with a dozen men backing him. Jeff wondered if Shortt had left a will. If he had, would his property go to Lawrence or Nikki? The answer, whichever it was, wouldn't help Jeff get out of town alive.

He kept crawling, raising up now and then to see where he was. Lawrence rode by again, and a moment later Jeff heard him call, "Brogan, you must have missed him."

Silence, then, with most of the lamps going out. The townsmen wanted no part of the hunt. Jeff reached the edge of Miles Rebus' property and cautiously raising his head, saw the preacher come out of the barn with Stilly and Quinn.

"Now will you get out of here?" Rebus demanded.

"I ain't satisfied," Stilly said. "We ain't been in the house. Maybe Steve Lawrence will take your word, but I won't."

"I don't want you in the house," Rebus said. "My wife's expecting a baby. If you go in and upset her, I'll break your neck."

"Tough talk for a preacher," Stilly said. "If there's a broken neck around here, it'll be yours. You're going into the house with us so we can watch you, or I'll cool you off for a while."

"Better go with us, Miles," Quinn said.

"Ardell's holed up somewhere and we're going to get him. You'll make it easier on your wife if you . . ."

He never finished his sentence. Miles hit him in the stomach. He was a powerful man and Quinn had not been expecting it. Quinn didn't go down, but he was helpless, bending forward and holding his middle as he gasped for breath that wouldn't come.

Miles whirled to face Stilly who had drawn his gun. Miles would have died in the next second if Jeff hadn't charged out of the ditch and brought his gun barrel down across the top of Stilly's head. Stilly folded at the knees and went down, out cold.

"You make a sound, mister," Jeff said to Quinn, "and you'll get it in the brisket."

"Don't shoot," Miles said sharply. "You'll bring the whole bunch down on us."

"Quinn will bring them down if he hollers," Jeff said. "I want him to know he's cold meat if he does. Where's their horses?"

"In the street," the preacher said.

"Some of them might be along," Jeff said. "Drag Stilly inside the barn so they won't see him if they show up. Quinn, I'm going to have my gun on you. Make a wrong move and you'll get it."

Jeff got Quinn by the coat collar and shoved him into the barn. Miles dragged

Stilly into a corner, then went back for the gun that had dropped from his hand when he'd fallen. He was barely in time, for Steve Lawrence rode back along the alley. Quinn stood in the barn doorway, still having trouble breathing.

Lawrence reined up and looked down at Quinn. He said, "I can't figure this out. He wouldn't leave town on foot, and we've got his horse. He's got to be around here somewhere."

Quinn stood with his side to Jeff who was three feet away behind the wall and thus hidden from Lawrence's sight. Quinn did not forget the gun in Jeff's hand. He said, "Ardell ain't here."

"Leave a man to watch," Miles said, "but stay out of my house. You've got no right to worry my wife."

"Sorry, Miles," Lawrence said. "I figured he'd come to you sure. I hate to accuse you of lying, but we've got to look in the house. That's one place we haven't been."

Jeff's gun jabbed Quinn's side. Quinn said, "He ain't there, Steve. We looked."

"He's likely in one of the sheds along the alley," Miles said. "You couldn't have made an adequate search in the dark."

"Naw, we've looked good enough." Lawrence glanced up at the sky. "If we don't find him pretty soon, he'll have a chance to sneak past us. The moon's gonna be covered purty soon, the way them clouds are boiling up."

"He might have got a horse at the livery stable," Quinn said.

"I put a man down there." Lawrence scratched his head. "It beats me. Well, I'll see what's going on across the street, but I think we'd have seen him if he'd gone to that side."

Lawrence rode away. Jeff said, "Miles, fetch the horses. I'm making a ride for it. I don't know how much trouble you'll have when Stilly comes to, but it'll be more trouble if they find me here. I wouldn't have come if I hadn't figured you'd be in trouble anyhow. That's what comes of being a friend of mine."

"I'd have had considerable trouble if you hadn't showed up when you did," Miles said bitterly. "Stilly would have shot me."

"Go fetch the horses," Jeff said.

Miles scratched the back of his neck. "I don't know about this, Jeff. You haven't got any chance trying to outrun them."

"I will with Quinn," Jeff said. "Get a move on."

The preacher walked away reluctantly. Quinn asked sullenly, "What's your game,

Ardell?"

"We're riding out together," Jeff said. "If anybody spots us, you'll tell them it's you and Stilly. With the clouds over the moon, you couldn't see real good, but you heard something yonder and you're taking a sashay out there to see about it."

"Won't work," Quinn said. "The boys'll get you."

"You better start praying they don't," Jeff said, "because I'll have a gun on you all the time."

When Miles returned with the horses, Jeff told him what he was going to do, then added, "If Lawrence shows up again, tell him Stilly and Quinn figure I struck out on foot."

"They know you wouldn't do that."

"Maybe it'll get them off your neck," Jeff said. "Better move Stilly out of the barn into the weeds."

He mounted, taking Stilly's horse, a bay gelding that was fast enough to give Jeff a chance if he had to make a run for it. Then he thought bitterly that it didn't make much difference how fast the horse was. It seemed to him that whatever he did was wrong, that time had run out for him. If the Wineglass men got on his tail again, he couldn't lead them to Tom Barren's house.

Quinn stepped up. Jeff said, "Lead out."

Quinn obeyed, Jeff following a few feet behind, his gun in his hand. They made a half circle of the town, riding slowly. When they reached the county road, a Wineglass man who had been stationed there called out, "Who is it?"

"Quinn and Stilly," Quinn shouted. "We figure he's got out of town."

"He ain't come this way," the cowhand yelled. "What do you think I've been doing?"

"Sleeping probably," Quinn said. "We got a glimpse of somebody running out here. If you'd been awake, you'd have nabbed him."

"Aw hell," the rider said indignantly. "Go ahead and look your damned head off. He ain't nowhere around here."

They jogged on. Jeff said softly, "You did real well, Quinn."

Quinn was silent for a time, then he muttered, "This is a hell of a mess. Did the boss really send for Sam Marks?"

"He did," Jeff said. "Marks murdered Lacey Dunbar today."

After that Quinn was silent. Jeff wondered how much loyalty was in Quinn and others like him who had worked for Wineglass before Slim Tarrant had started rodding the outfit. That was something Jeff would find out before long.

"Get off," Jeff said. "You're walking back."

Quinn obeyed, saying nothing. Jeff went on, leading Quinn's horse. He had put enough distance between him and town so that he knew he would make it to Barren's place without having the Wineglass crew on his tail.

Nikki and his folks would be safe for several hours, but what about tomorrow?

Chapter XX

The coming of the Ardell wagon to Tom Barren's ranch in the middle of the night did not make Barren happy. He would have felt differently if circumstances had been different. But happy or not, there was nothing he could do except to welcome them.

He carried Matthew into the house and laid him on the couch; he gave Nancy and Nikki his bed, cautioned them about lighting a lamp, put the team away, and returned to his blankets in the aspens.

Barren had been asleep, but now he was wide awake and restless. He was afraid to smoke, knowing that it would give him away if Marks were looking for him, so he sat with his back against an aspen trunk. He was afraid, more afraid than he had ever been in his life.

The terror gave him the feeling of having skim milk in his veins. He had expected Sam Marks to come to him before now and claim the $2,000 he had been offered. Barren had thought he could buy safety, but Marks hadn't come and Lacey Dunbar was dead, killed as Tom Barren might be killed before this was over.

Tom Barren was not a man to wallow in self-pity. He had always been a dreamer, and he was certain that it was no fault of his which had kept his accomplishments from keeping up with his dreams.

If luck had been with him as it had been with Ben Shortt the last three years, he'd be in the same enviable position Shortt was in now. At least he would have pushed Floyd Deems and Red O'Toole off the creek below him. Maybe some of the others, too. He'd own three times as many head of cattle as he did, and he'd have a crew of men working for him instead of doing everything himself.

But he'd never been lucky. Something had always gone wrong. Disease. Hard times and low prices. A bank loan which had come due before he was ready to pay. Drouth and poor graze that had forced him to dispose of some heifers which he would otherwise have kept. His Shorthorns had been disappointing. He had paid a high price for the bulls and then found that Shorthorns were not as good rustlers as

Herefords.

Gradually his faith in his destiny re-asserted itself and he began to see the bright side of the picture. Sam Marks would show up tomorrow for his money and leave the country. If Jeff was killed tonight, Barren would find a way to get rid of Matthew. Then Nancy would turn to him because she had no one else.

Nikki and Shortt would make up. Nikki would be indebted to Barren after he had given her a place to stay. She'd get Shortt off his neck. He would move to the Rafter A with Nancy. Or he could stay here and claim the ranches on down the creek.

The sound of a horse coming in across the grass broke into his thinking and brought the old fears rushing back. He rose, his Winchester in his hand. For a time the moon had been covered by clouds, but it was clear now. He watched the rider come down the mesa hill and cross the creek, and then he saw it was Jeff.

Barren was momentarily jarred, having been certain Jeff would never leave Wine-glass alive. Recovering, he called, "Jeff." He stepped out into the moonlight and waited until Jeff reached him. He said, "I didn't think I'd ever see you again."

"It was tight," Jeff said. "Shortt's dead.

Steve Lawrence had the crew in town trying to turn me up. By this time he knows I got away, so I'm guessing we'll have a visit."

"Why in hell didn't you go somewhere else?" Barren asked harshly. "You knew your folks and Nikki are here."

"I don't have to stay," Jeff said. "but it's my guess the Wineglass boys will think I'm here and they'll show up whether I am or not. If they do, you'll need my gun."

It took a moment for Barren to work into his thinking the fact that Shortt was dead, not Jeff, and when he did, he decided luck was finally on his side. Everything would be different with Shortt gone, for he'd had money, and money had given him power. Jeff, having neither, would be easier to deal with.

"I'll need your gun, all right," Barren said, "but it'll be a cinch to take care of Wineglass now. Steve Lawrence is a poor excuse of a man compared to Ben Shortt. Why don't you put your horse up and sleep in the hay mow?"

"You going to stay up?" Jeff asked.

"You bet I am," Barren answered.

"Then I'll roll in," Jeff said. "It's been a night."

"It'll be daylight soon," Barren said. "I'll send your mother and Nikki down the creek

227

to Floyd Deems's place. They'll be safer there than here if we have a fight."

"Good idea," Jeff said, and rode on to the corral.

Barren slipped back into the aspens and waited until it was full daylight. He made a circle of the clearing as he had been doing every morning, but with less care than usual. Now, knowing that Ben Shortt was dead, he was filled with a confidence he had not felt for a long time.

He regretted not killing Shortt himself the night he had gone to Wineglass, but he had not realized before how completely Ben Shortt had dominated his own thinking. He was not a man who could fasten blame upon himself, so he pinned it on Shortt. With the man dead, nothing could hold Tom Barren back. Nothing!

He went into the house and built a fire. He fixed breakfast, letting the Ardells and Nikki sleep as long as they could. Then he woke them, wanting to get the two women out of the house as soon as he could.

When he told Nikki her grandfather was dead, she simply nodded. If she felt any grief, she did not show it. She asked, "Jeff?"

"He's asleep in the barn," Barren said.

As soon as Nancy finished her breakfast, she took a bowl of oatmeal mush and a cup of coffee to Matthew, but he was able to eat only a few bites. He was so tired he didn't want to sit up, so Nancy moved the pillows away from his back and covered him with a quilt. The morning was still chilly, and there were enough clouds in the sky to keep the day from turning hot.

"I'll harness your team and hook up," Barren said to Nancy when she returned to the kitchen. "I want you and Nikki to go to Floyd Deems's place. I think they're gone, but you can stay in the house. You'll be safer there than you will be here."

"You expect me to leave Matthew?" she asked incredulously.

"That's exactly what I expect," Barren said. "Matthew's too tired to be moved right away. Besides, he's a man and he can still pull a trigger. His place is here and that's where he'd want to be."

Nancy's face turned stubborn. "I won't go."

"It's what Jeff wants," Barren said. "He'll look after Matthew. He can do anything for Matthew you can."

Still she stood there, shaking her head, her mouth drawn into a tight line against her teeth. Impatient now, Barren said, "You're going if I have to tie you and carry you out to the wagon. We're in for a hell of a fight and the presence of two women in the house is a handicap, not an asset. Besides, Jeff doesn't want Nikki here where she might get killed by a stray bullet."

He strode out of the kitchen, irritated by Nancy's stubbornness. For a moment his confidence was shaken. He remembered the last time he had been at the Rafter A and how he had always been so certain Nancy loved him, only to have that certainty destroyed.

He went on out to the barn and harnessed the Ardell team, the irritation leaving him. Nancy would need a little time after Matthew's death, but she would come to him. Time! The word kept repeating itself in his mind. That was what she needed, time. He'd get the women out of the way, then he'd shoot Matthew and blame it on Sam Marks. By the time Jeff woke and came out of the barn, Marks would probably be here.

He drove the wagon to the back door. The women had finished the dishes. They got into the wagon and left without any more argument. Barren remained by the back door until they disappeared.

Suddenly he was possessed by a feeling that time was running out on him. Jeff might wake up and come into the house. Or Steve Lawrence might show up with the

Wineglass crew. Not that Barren worried about it. Lawrence wasn't worth worrying about. It was just that Barren wanted it finished before they got here.

He went into the house and crossed the kitchen to the front room where Matthew lay asleep on the couch, an arm thrown over his face. Barren stood looking down, hating him. Suddenly it occurred to Barren that he was more like Ben Shortt than he had realized.

Shortt should have been Matthew's friend, but he hadn't been. He had hated Matthew just as Barren did, but for different reasons. Or were their reasons different? Was it because of what Matthew was, because he had qualities that were missing in both Shortt and Barren, because other men liked and respected Matthew?

No, Barren thought, and was angry because these thoughts entered his mind. Whatever Shortt's reasons had been, Barren's were different. It was simply that he wanted Nancy and he could never have her as long as she was married to Matthew.

Barren drew his gun and lifted it slowly. He listened for steps in the kitchen or on the front porch. Jeff might come in. No, there wasn't a sound of any kind. Just the silence he had lived with for twelve years, twelve years of being alone without a woman. By God, it was time he had one.

The hand with the gun stopped. Then it began rising again. This would be as easy as stepping on a bug. But once more the hand stopped. Barren felt his heart pound, felt the sweat stream down his face. He'd better have a look at Jeff. If Jeff caught him at this, he was a dead man.

He shoved his gun into the holster and went out through the front. He started toward the barn, then stopped. A man was standing at the edge of the aspens above the house. When Barren looked at him, the man motioned to him.

Sam Marks!

For a moment a terrible fear filled his spine with a thousand squirming things. Marks motioned again, and Barren turned and walked toward him, his courage surging back. Marks didn't aim to kill him or he would have shot him where he stood. No, Marks had come for his money.

As Barren crossed the meadow, he decided he wouldn't tell Marks about Shortt's death. Marks killed only for money. If he knew Shortt wouldn't pay him for Jeff's murder, he might not consider Barren's offer big enough to make it worthwhile.

Marks smiled amiably as Barren stopped

a few feet away from him. Barren said, "I hear you got Dunbar."

"I got him," Marks said.

"Jeff Ardell was in the house," Barren said. "If you'd waited a few seconds, you could have got him, too."

Marks shrugged. "I never wait after I've killed a man. Got the money you were talking about?"

"Right here." Barren drew an envelope filled with greenbacks from his pocket. He jerked his head at the barn. "Ardell's asleep. This time you'd better wait."

Marks's smile widened. "So he's here. Well, Mr. Barren, count out half of that money and give it to me. The other half you keep in the envelope."

This puzzled Barren, but he obeyed. He wasn't going to argue with a man like Sam Marks. He handed Marks the money and put the other bills into the envelope and slipped it back into his coat.

"I made an offer," Barren said. "It's still good. I don't know why you don't want to earn the rest of this."

"I made a bargain with Ben Shortt, Mr. Barren." Marks's lips curled as he said *Mister.* "I always keep a bargain, so I can't take the money you offered me to keep you alive."

Marks lifted his gun from the holster, a slow deliberate move, amused eyes on Barren's face. Then Barren realized he was going to die. He had not bought safety as he had supposed. He had a gun. He could draw it faster than Marks was raising his.

But he simply stood there, his mouth gaping open. He was only a few seconds from death. He had never killed a man. He had always assured himself that he could, but now he realized he was incapable of it.

There was something wrong with him. He was weak. That was the reason he had not killed Ben Shortt when he had a chance. It was why he had not killed Matthew a few minutes ago.

All he had ever done was run when the blue chip was down. He let out a cry, a strange sobbing sound, and started to turn to run. Marks's gun roared, Barren was jolted and slammed back, and it seemed to him he was spiraling down through a slanting dark tunnel that was without a bottom. Then Marks's gun roared again and Barren fell, all feeling and all knowledge gone from him.

"I took your money to kill Ardell," Marks said, the smile remaining on his lips. "I told you I always keep my bargains. I'll keep this one."

Chapter XXI

The conviction that this would be the day of decision had been in Jeff's mind when he'd gone to sleep. The sound of the wagon leaving with Nikki and his mother woke him, but still he lay there, staring at the ceiling with its glittering stars of sunlight where the shingles didn't quite meet. The first thought that stirred his mind was the same one that had been there when he'd gone to sleep: the Wineglass crew would come today.

Jeff had slept only a short time and the temptation was great to close his eyes. He would drop off immediately if he did, but he couldn't afford to be trapped up here. He rose and shook the chaff off his back. He had thought that when Ben Shortt died, everything would automatically be all right. Now he realized he couldn't have been more wrong.

He went down the ladder, his Winchester in his hand, knowing there was nothing to do but wait. He stepped into the sunlight, breathing the cool morning air. He started toward the house, gaze sweeping the creek as he wondered where Sam Marks was, then he turned his gaze toward the aspens above the meadows and stopped abruptly.

Tom Barren was talking to a stranger. It could be Marks. Jeff didn't have the slightest idea what the man looked like. This fellow could be some drifter who had stopped to ask something. Jeff decided it wasn't Marks, or Barren wouldn't be standing there talking to him. But maybe Barren didn't know who the man was.

The stranger and Barren seemed friendly enough one second, the next the stranger drew his gun and cut Barren down. It happened so unexpectedly that Jeff simply stood there, shocked.

It was Sam Marks! There wasn't the slightest doubt in Jeff's mind as he raised his Winchester. He squeezed the trigger just as the man glanced toward the house and saw him. Marks dropped to the ground, the bullet going over his head.

The man had used his Colt to kill Barren. Now he threw a shot at Jeff, but the distance was too far to be accurate with a revolver. He missed, the slug digging up dirt ten feet in front of Jeff. Apparently realizing that he couldn't do anything with his Colt, he dived frantically toward the nearest aspen.

Jeff fired again, and missed, then Marks was behind the aspen, flat on his belly. The tree was too small to give him adequate protection. Jeff could see the points of his shoulders flat on the ground on both sides of the trunk, so apparently Marks had his nose buried in the dirt behind the aspen.

Jeff let go a third shot that knocked bark off one side of the tree trunk. It was close, but he missed the shoulder. He cursed himself for missing twice when Marks was in the open. He thought briefly of Lacey Dunbar, and of Barren shot down when he apparently thought Marks was a drifting stranger. If he let Marks get away, he would probably never have another chance at him.

Jeff began to run across the meadow, keeping his eyes on the aspen. As long as Marks lay there with his nose in the dirt, he wasn't a threat. But Marks must know he couldn't stay there.

Jeff had covered half the distance between them when Marks showed his face on one side of the tree trunk. Jeff stopped and fired, but Marks snapped his head back in time, and Jeff went on, running hard.

Marks jumped to his feet and threw a shot with his revolver that was close, but he wasn't a man to stand and fight. He wheeled and ran, taking a zig-zag course and making use of every tree he could so that he was constantly darting into view and then out again. He made a difficult target, so Jeff didn't stop. He was closing the distance between them, for he was taking a direct course and Marks was steadily losing, zig-zagging the way he was.

It occurred to Jeff that Marks had a horse farther up the slope. Although Jeff was steadily cutting down the distance, he probably wouldn't catch up with Marks before he reached his horse.

Jeff stopped and dropped to one knee, still several yards short of where Tom Barren lay. Jeff raised his rifle, his right elbow on his knee, and taking a rest this way, drew back the hammer. He hesitated, finger tight against the trigger. When Marks scurried into the open, Jeff squeezed off his shot.

Marks stumbled as if a hand had reached up out of the ground and grabbed him by an ankle and tripped him. He fell headlong and rolled over, his revolver dropping from slack fingers. Jeff was up and running the instant Marks started to fall. When he reached Marks, he saw that no one would ever fear Sam Marks again.

Marks was alive, but he didn't make any

effort to pick up the gun which lay a few inches from his right hand. Standing over him, Jeff asked, "You're Sam Marks, aren't you?"

"Yeah, I'm Sam Marks. I've been careful for nine years, then I forget for one minute and you plug me." He closed his eyes, both hands fisting against his shirt, a trickle of blood running from his mouth over his chin. "I'm hit hard, ain't I?"

"Hard enough," Jeff said.

"I don't want to die," Marks said. "By God, I guess I'm afraid."

"You think Lacey Dunbar wanted to die? Or Tom Barren?" Marks didn't answer. Jeff asked, "Why did you plug Barren?"

Marks's teeth were clenched, his lips squeezed so tightly they were white. Finally he said hoarsely, "He paid me a thousand dollars to get you. I took it 'cause Shortt had already told me to plug you."

He opened his eyes and shut them again as agony wrenched his body, then he whispered, "Barren tried to stay alive by buying his life for another thousand, but Shortt had already paid me to kill him. I'd made a bargain, so I couldn't take it."

Looking down at Marks, Jeff wondered what kind of man this was who could talk about killing a man as easily as most men

239

talk about bringing down a buck. At first glance Jeff had thought Marks was hardly more than a boy, but now he saw the killer was older than he had supposed. Still, he bore no resemblance to the mental picture Jeff had formed of how a paid killer would look.

Marks's eyes flicked open. "I always keep a bargain," he said thickly, "but this is one I can't keep."

That was all. He died, staring at the sky, afraid of the death he had given so many other men. Jeff picked up Marks's revolver and turning, walked back down the slope.

Jeff knelt beside Barren. The man was dead as Jeff had been sure he would be. He pulled Barren's gun from his holster, and rose. He saw a rifle leaning against an aspen and took it. Probably Marks's Winchester, he thought. He walked back across the meadow to the house, carrying the rifle and two revolvers.

Why would Barren pay Marks to kill him, Jeff wondered? He'd had plenty of chance to do it himself, but he had posed as a friend. Jeff went into the house, completely puzzled. He found Matthew awake and worried.

"What was all the shooting for?" Matthew asked.

Jeff pulled up a chair and told Matthew about it, then asked, "Why would Tom hire Marks to kill me? It doesn't make sense."

"No, it doesn't," Matthew admitted, "but he tried to kill me this morning. He thought I was asleep. I had an arm over my eyes, but I gave myself a peep hole. I had my gun under the quilt. If he'd got his gun level and ready to shoot, I'd have let him have it. He never did. He just stood there, kind of like he was listening. He'd raise his gun a little, stop, and raise it again. Finally he shoved it back into the holster and walked out."

Jeff shook his head, more puzzled than ever. He hadn't trusted Barren, yet it was hard to believe he had almost been guilty of the murder of two men he had claimed as friends. Jeff remembered Lacey Dunbar saying that no one knew what went on in Barren's head. Dunbar had been right, but it was no explanation.

"Tom wasn't much man," Matthew said thoughtfully. "He was always one to talk big and plan big, and he worked hard, but he never got to where he wanted to go."

"He claimed he wasn't in the rustling," Jeff said, "and Lacey didn't think he was, but I'm not so sure about it."

"He could have been," Matthew said. "He

241

was smart, some ways, and a plain damned fool in others."

Jeff looked at his father who was staring at the ceiling, his mind still on Barren. Jeff suspected that Matthew had a theory as to why Barren had tried to kill him, but Matthew didn't offer to share it and Jeff didn't press him.

"Ben Shortt's dead," Jeff said.

Matthew turned startled eyes on him. "How did it happen?"

Jeff told him, adding, "I figure we'll see some of the Wineglass boys today. Nothing to do but wait, I guess."

"It's not over," Matthew said. "Ben kept tromping on Steve Lawrence for years, and now that Ben's gone, Steve will have his chance for glory. Money, too, if he can grab Wineglass."

"That's the way I figure it," Jeff said. "Steve may decide he's ten feet tall."

Jeff was silent, looking at Matthew and thinking about him, and suddenly he realized that he and his father were closer at this moment than they had been for years. He burst out, "Dad, we've both been wrong. When you got hurt, you pulled back into a shell and wouldn't leave the ranch, figuring you weren't good for anything. I should have made you. Taken you and your chair to church. And to town on Saturday afternoons."

"But instead of that," Matthew said bitterly, "I stayed home, so folks got to thinking I was as good as dead. In a way I'm to blame for old Ben running wild."

"I didn't mean that . . ."

"Well, you should have if you didn't," Matthew said tartly. "Now I'll tell you something, Jeff. If we live through this, which I'm not sure we will, I'm going to get away from the Rafter A. I'll be like a man rising from the grave."

He turned his head to look out of the window. He swore incredulously as if he could not believe what he was seeing. He said, "Jeff, if you killed Ben last night, I'm looking at a dead man riding a horse."

Chapter XXII

Jeff got up to look through the window. What he saw hit him just as it had hit Matthew. The Wineglass bunch was coming down the mesa hill, Ben Shortt leading them, his left arm in a sling. Steve Lawrence rode beside him, Brogan and Stilly and the rest strung out behind. Ten of them, too many to fight with any chance of winning. If Steve Lawrence had been leading them, there might have been a chance, but with Shortt in command there was none.

Jeff heard a wagon behind the house. Running to the back door, he looked out. Nikki and his mother! He swore angrily, thinking that this was the worst thing that could happen.

He stepped through the door, calling, "Get inside. Both of you. Quick." They obeyed. He asked, "Why didn't you stay at Deems's ranch?"

"They're gone and the house is burned to

the ground," Nikki said. She stood very straight, her head tipped back, and she added, "We should never have gone in the first place. The only reason we did was because Tom Barren said we'd be liabilities. But we won't. We can both shoot."

"Stay inside." He whirled and ran into the front room. Shortt and his men had forded the creek and were coming in across the meadow. Jeff was almost to the front door when Matthew said, "Pull my couch to the door, Jeff."

Jeff hesitated, staring at his father. He saw an eagerness in Matthew's eyes he had not seen for a long time, a miracle of sorts that stripped years from him. He would be better to die this morning than to live with the knowledge that he was useless, unable to do a man's job when the chips were down.

"All right," Jeff said.

Taking hold of the foot of the couch, Jeff dragged it to the door so that Matthew's head and shoulders, propped up with pillows, were in the doorway. His gun was in his hand, lying across his stomach. He grinned at Jeff and winked.

"We'll see, Jeff," Matthew said. "We'll see."

Jeff glanced back at his mother and Nikki who had come into the front room and stood a few feet from the couch. "Stay back," he said. "Away from the windows and the door."

He stepped over the couch and crossed the porch, easing his gun in the holster and letting it settle back. The Wineglass men reined up, dust whipping around them in a red cloud. Jeff had a bad moment then, not knowing what Shortt's orders had been. He had to keep his eyes on Shortt, but some of the men farther back, Stilly and Brogan at least, could pull their guns and cut him down before he caught a hint of movement.

But that was not the way Shortt meant to play it. He swung down, keeping a hand on the saddle horn for support, then he motioned for Lawrence to dismount. The dust had been swept away by the breeze. Jeff could see every man clearly now, then his gaze returned to Shortt. He had no idea what the old man planned to do, but suddenly he realized that Shortt was a sick man, his face as gray as death, his seventy years pressing against him.

From the doorway Matthew called, "You bastards keep your hands away from your gun butts. I'll kill you if you don't."

"You couldn't kill nobody." Shortt tried to shout as he had always done when he wanted to override his opposition, but he lacked the physical strength. The words came out hardly more than a hoarse whisper.

"I killed Slim Tarrant and Curly Jones," Matthew said. "These coyotes will die just as easy."

"Sam Marks shot Tom Barren this morning," Jeff said, "and I shot Marks. Isn't that enough to satisfy you, Ben?"

Shortt didn't answer. He looked past Jeff at Matthew. He released his grip on the saddle horn and took a step forward, swaying a little, the corners of his mouth twitching.

Shortt took another step, lurching like a drunk, then he said, "I came for my granddaughter. Is she here?"

Nikki stepped into view behind Matthew. "I'm here, Grandpa. I'm not going back. Don't you know that yet?"

Again he moved forward, motioning to the men behind him. "Cut 'em down. All of 'em."

But now Nikki had a rifle in her hands. She said, "Don't try it, any of you."

Jeff strode toward Shortt, saying, "You've got to the end of the trail, Ben. Give me your gun."

"I'll kill you, God damn you."

Again Shortt tried to throw his words out

in a great bellow, but the strength still wasn't in him. Jeff kept going. Shortt reached for his gun. He lifted it from leather, then it seemed to be too heavy and all of his straining could not bring it up another inch. Jeff put a hand out and took the gun from Shortt.

Shortt cursed. He tried to strike Jeff, but he couldn't raise his fist above his shoulders. His knees gave and he sprawled forward into the dust which rose up around him in a brick-red cloud. He put the palms of his hands against the ground and tried to raise himself, but he could not, he reached out with both hands and clawed the dirt in a futile effort to pull himself forward, but his great body didn't move an inch. There was no movement at all except that of his outstretched fingers which made wavy lines in the dust.

For one short moment he manged to lift his head a few inches out of the dirt, then it fell back. He had nothing to drive him now except his hate. All the magnificent strength that had built Wineglass was gone from him. Ben Shortt was nothing more than a mass of helpless, quivering flesh.

Stooping, Jeff turned him over on his back. He was laboring for every breath, his tremendous chest rising and falling, his empty hands flung out on both sides of him. He was staring at the sky, but Jeff doubted that he saw anything. Then his mouth sagged open, his liver-brown lips falling away from his yellow teeth. Spit drooled from both sides of his mouth to flow down his unshaven cheeks, and on into the dirt where it made little balls of mud.

There was this brief interval of time when life seemed to stand still, when there had been no movement but that of Jeff turning Shortt over on his back, an interval of time when shock held the watchers in a strait jacket. Nikki was the first to recover. She cried out, and climbing over the couch, ran to Shortt and cradled his head in her lap.

"Hold it back there," Matthew called. "I'll kill the first man who reaches for his gun."

Jeff straightened and stepped back, his gaze sweeping the Wineglass riders. He said, "How about it, Stilly? Brogan? Riley?" He motioned toward Shortt. "If you die now, it'll be for nothing."

Stilly looked at Lawrence. "There's just two of 'em, Steve, and one of 'em is an old man who couldn't hit nothing."

"He hit Curly Jones and Slim Tarrant." Jeff's gun was in his hand now. "You make a play, Stilly, and I'll blow your head off and I'll get Steve. You figure it's worth it?"

"No," Lawrence said. "Nothing to die for now." He looked at Jeff. "Is there a wagon here?"

So the mouse remained a mouse, Jeff thought, and said, "Behind the house."

"Fetch it around, Stilly," Lawrence ordered. "We'll take Ben back to Wineglass."

Without a word Stilly wheeled his horse and rode across the meadow toward the creek, all the others but Quinn following. Lawrence yelled, "What's the matter with you? Do what I tell you or you're fired."

Stilly looked back. "You can't fire men who ain't working for you," he said, and rode on.

Quinn dismounted and walked to where Lawrence stood. "Wineglass don't have a crew no more, Steve. Just me'n the cook and a few old hands who are at the cow camps. I reckon it'll be up to Nikki to hire a new crew. Wineglass belongs to her."

Lawrence's face turned red. He started to say something, choked, and then got on his horse and followed the others. Jeff holstered his gun and put a hand on Nikki's shoulder. He said, "He's dead, isn't he?"

"Yes," she said. "He's dead. When he was in Denver he went to a doctor because he'd been having chest pains. The doctor told him his heart would quit if he didn't take care of himself. He could have lived a long time, but he killed himself."

"I'll get the wagon," Quinn said. "Miss Nikki, you'd best come home. A ranch don't run itself."

Nikki didn't answer. She sat motionless, still holding Shortt's head on her lap. "I'll bring her," Jeff said, and walked around the house with Quinn. "What happened? I thought I shot him last night."

"You busted his arm all to hell," Quinn said. "Hank Dolan hollered that you'd shot him, so we took out after you, figuring he was dead. After you was gone, Ben lighted a lamp and damned if Hank didn't try to shoot him, but he wasn't no part of a man. Ben got him. He hollered for the cook and the cook put a bandage on that arm. Then Mick Hennessy woke up from that whack you gave him. Ben sent him to town to fetch us back, which he done."

"Ben came here, figuring to get me?" Jeff asked.

"I reckon," Quinn said, "though he didn't tell nobody what he aimed to do. I think mostly he wanted Nikki back. Taking her away from him was the one thing he couldn't forgive you for. He lost a lot of blood from that arm and he should of stayed in bed, but hell, talking to him was a waste of wind. How he stayed on his horse all the way across the mesa was a mystery to me."

Jeff drove the wagon to the front of the house, and helped Quinn lift Shortt's body into the bed. Nikki brought a quilt from the house and spread it over the body.

"I'll go back, Jeff," Nikki said. "I owe him that much. We'll bury him on Wineglass. That's the way he'd want it. Quinn, you go to town and tell Miles Rebus."

"Go with her, Jeff," Matthew called from the doorway. "We'll be all right here till you get back."

Jeff hesitated, looking at his father and then his mother who stood beside the couch. He nodded and gave Nikki a hand to the seat. He climbed up and sat beside her and took the lines. Quinn had already started for town. Jeff turned back once and waved, then Nikki laid a hand on his arm.

"I don't want Wineglass," she said. "I want to live with you on the Rafter A. What will we do?"

He looked at her, not knowing what to say. In time she might change her mind and regret giving up Wineglass. He said finally, "Dad's changed. He's alive again. It's the only good thing that came out of this mess. If he can find a good foreman, he could run the Rafter A from his wheel chair, it would be good for him to have some responsibility."

"You?" she asked. "You'd come to Wineglass?"

Jeff nodded. "I want to be wherever you are, and looks like Wineglass is yours. You'll need a foreman, too."

"I need a husband," she said, "but there's no reason why you can't be both."

"Why no," he said. "No reason at all."

ABOUT THE AUTHOR

Wayne D. Overholser has won three Golden Spur awards from the Western Writers of America and has a long list of fine Western titles to his credit. He was born in Pomeroy, Washington, and attended the University of Montana, University of Oregon, and the University of Southern California before becoming a public school teacher and principal in various Oregon communities. He began writing for Western pulp magazines in 1936 and within a couple of years was a regular contributor to Street & Smith's *Western Story* and Fiction House's *Lariat Story Magazine. Buckaroo's Code* (1948) was his first Western novel and remains one of his best. In the 1950s and 1960s, having retired from academic work to concentrate on writing, he would publish as many as four books a year under his own name or a pseudonym, most prominently as Joseph Wayne. *The Bitter Night, The Lone*

Deputy, and *The Violent Land* are among the finest of the early Overholser titles. He was asked by William MacLeod Raine, that dean among Western writers, to complete his last novel after Raine's death. Some of Overholser's most rewarding novels were actually collaborations with other Western writers: *Colorado Gold* with Chad Merriman and *Showdown at Stony Creek* with Lewis B. Patten. Overholser's Western novels, no matter under what name they have been published, are based on a solid knowledge of the history and customs of the American frontier West, particularly when set in his two favorite Western states, Oregon and Colorado. When it comes to his characters, he writes with skill, an uncommon sensitivity, and a consistently vivid and accurate vision of a way of life unique in human history.

We hope you have enjoyed this Large Print book. Other Thorndike, Wheeler, Kennebec, and Chivers Press Large Print books are available at your library or directly from the publishers.

For information about current and upcoming titles, please call or write, without obligation, to:

Publisher
Thorndike Press
295 Kennedy Memorial Drive
Waterville, ME 04901
Tel. (800) 223-1244

or visit our Web site at:

http://gale.cengage.com/thorndike

OR

Chivers Large Print
published by BBC Audiobooks Ltd
St James House, The Square
Lower Bristol Road
Bath BA2 3SB
England
Tel. +44(0) 800 136919
email: bbcaudiobooks@bbc.co.uk
www.bbcaudiobooks.co.uk

All our Large Print titles are designed for easy reading, and all our books are made to last.